THE
ROSE
THIEVES

THE
ROSE
THIEVES

Heidi Jon Schmidt

HARCOURT BRACE JOVANOVICH, PUBLISHERS

San Diego New York London

Requests for permission to make copies of any
part of the work should be mailed to:
Permissions Department
Harcourt Brace Jovanovich, Publishers
Orlando, Florida 32887

Library of Congress Cataloging-in-Publication Data
Schmidt, Heidi Jon.
The rose thieves/by Heidi Jon Schmidt.
p. cm.
PS3561.C51554R6   1990
813'.54—dc20   89-26918

Printed in the United States of America

First edition
A   B   C   D   E

ACKNOWLEDGMENTS

"In the Zoot Car" and "Nonchalant" (under the title "Chez
Sophie") first appeared in *The Atlantic*,
"Shoe" first appeared in *Grand Street*,
"The Honored Guest" first appeared in *Yankee*,
"Audrey: Keeper of the Flame" first appeared
in *The Boston Globe Magazine*, and
"Katie Vanderwald" first appeared in *The Agni Review*.

The author wishes to acknowledge with gratitude the
Massachusetts Artists Foundation, the Ingram-Merrill
Foundation, the Fine Arts Work Center in Province-
town, the Copernicus Society (the Michener Award),
the Corporation of Yaddo, and the Connecticut
Commission on the Arts, whose support
made it possible to write this book.

CONTENTS

For my mother, my father,
Laura Ann, Willi, Martha, and John

THE
ROSE
THIEVES

The Art of Conversation

" 'By-the-bye, what became of the baby?' said the Cat. 'I'd
nearly forgotten to ask.'
" 'It turned into a pig,' Alice answered very quietly, just as
if the Cat had come back in a natural way.
" 'I thought it would,' said the Cat, and vanished again."
My mother stopped reading, not that she had finished the
chapter, but we heard my father's guests leaving by the back
door. She watched from the bathroom window as they went up
the hill to the driveway, two blocky, hunting-coated farmers
who'd come from the valley to sell us a side of beef.

We almost never had visitors; we were new in town, and Ma
didn't like anyone. The doctors and their wives were concerned
mostly with football and antiques, the farmers were full of prej-
udice and superstition. The hedonism of the summer people
(psychiatrists and editors up from New York) and the snobbery
of our only real neighbors, an exiled White Russian couple who
intended to raise pheasants on the land next to ours, were too
repellent even to discuss—when their names came up, Ma just
made a sour mouth. If a car pulled into the driveway, she'd run
up the stairs, telling my father to say she had a headache, and
read *Alice in Wonderland* to me. We'd been through three chap-
ters that afternoon, with Ma marking intermissions by listen-

ing, at the stairwell, for my father's laugh. It was far too hearty. What had possessed him to let them stay so long? Now she went down, with me trailing like a dinghy in her wake, listening as her voice dropped to its iciest depth to question him, watching as she cleared the beer glasses from the table with enraged efficiency, as, running water in the sink, sponge in hand, she changed her mind and (inspired by the Dutchess' pot-hurling cook?) punctuated her volley of grievances by throwing the glasses, one by one, at his head.

She was not comfortable in the world, too large for it, perhaps, or too small. A trip to the grocer's was daunting as a safari for her, so chimerical were the local housewives and cashiers. At home, if my father was at work, she wouldn't answer the door at all. We had a wonderfully rich and various life all our own, she would have said, with our books, our garden, our imaginary games: we pictured ourselves Indians when we walked in the woods, settlers when we sat at the fire. If Ma was reading Jane Austen, she'd tell me about the Bennets and how I'd grow up to be just like them; when she read Proust, she promised we'd move to Paris, become demoiselles of the demimonde. We needed none of reality—Ma felt it was crushingly dull.

Old women, small children, the deathly ill, and members of various religious orders were exempt from the general censure. When the Congregational pastor called to say he and his wife usually welcomed Brimfield's new residents at this time of year (it was October, the lull before the holiday rush) and asked could they visit us some afternoon for tea, Ma answered emphatically, "Yes."

This, like every other slightly unusual occurrence in our lives, became a Great Event. They were coming on a Wednesday, so my father would be away and there was no one to damp our anticipation. We saw ourselves first as Puritans lifting the corn-cake from our stony hearth to serve the black-clad, eagle-faced Reverend, then (it seemed a shame to waste flour on something

2

as dry as corncake, when we could have sponge cake filled with chestnut paste, raspberry jam, and whipped cream) as Parisians welcoming a soigné monseigneur. Ma sketched the scene for me: the charmingly erudite cleric, who by "tea" would mean "port," really (we were skimming across the Channel toward a more Trollopian scheme), would make conversation with us, all flash and parry, laughter and wit, skewering his parish of rich women, detailing his travels in the Levant.

Fledgling socialites, we studied with ardor. Ma taught me to walk like a lady (silently; nothing must distract from my beauty) and to say (always to the lady first), "May I pour you out some tea?" "Isn't the weather fine?" I repeated after her, and (the words—I couldn't yet mimic her satirical tone) "Yes, I certainly agree."

It began to seem as if our cavernous, beamed, and paneled living room would magically become, when the Reverend entered it, a gilt and satin parlor overlooking (what did it matter?) the Thames, or the Seine. So that the talk might do justice to the view, Ma lectured me on the art of conversation. "The sky tonight looks like . . ." she'd say, and I'd search for the perfect analogy, trying phrase after phrase until one seemed to strike the heart of the vision, showing not just how it looked but the way it made me feel.

We nearly forgot about the Reverend in the pleasure of preparing for him. The day of his visit dawned under a small, anxious cloud: we were still ourselves, still living in that dullest of times, the present. The visit could not be what we had hoped.

"Inviting themselves over . . ." said Ma, as she cracked a definitive egg. "I never heard of such a thing."

But as she whipped the whites to a froth, as they took on their own billowing life (like thunderheads . . . Arabian tents . . . a swan's rear end), she took courage, and by teatime she was a woman I'd never seen before, a Young Wife out of a magazine, in lipstick and cherry-red wool. She seemed taller, straighter, her smile direct and suddenly magnetic, as if her misanthropic agony had only been stage fright, mastered now the curtain was rising. Snapping her earrings off, replacing them, she ran on stockinged feet (the cake would fall if we didn't tiptoe, she said) from the bathroom, where she checked her face in the mirror, to the kitchen, where she checked the cake in the oven, and back.

"Now, Katie," she said, kneeling—falling to her knees, really, in her narrow skirt—on the carpet before me. "I want you to be very good and grown up and not get in the way." She plucked at my curls, fluffing them the way she'd plumped the sofa pillows a minute before. It was part of her new persona—she was treating me like a child!

"Of course I'll be good," I said, with such bitter dignity that she remembered herself and became naturally maternal for a moment, gentle and full of sense.

"You'll be a brilliant conversationalist," she said, straightening my collar. "Remember, it's just like talking to me. Ask them about things they're interested in, or tell them things that are interesting to you. The way we talk about *Alice in Wonderland.*"

"Off with their heads!" said I. It was her favorite line, ruthlessly repeated and often in the Red Queen's rapid-fire style, but sometimes (when, for instance, my father had angered her) slowly, musingly, and as if there were a guillotine in the next room.

She gave a shout of laughter—we were kindred, confidantes, conspirators again. I was her best friend—her only friend in the world.

The mantel clock chimed its ominous prelude, then the hour: four o'clock. The Reverend Twilling was due to arrive, but we waited five, then ten minutes with no sign.

"Took a wrong turn, I suppose," Ma said gaily, as if one must expect the occasional guest to be swallowed by the woods. We lived ten miles from church and town, and people tended to turn back halfway because they couldn't believe that the rutted dirt roads, which forked over plank bridges and climbed through brushy forest only to drop toward a beaver swamp peopled by legions of limbless trees, would lead them to anyone's home.

"I suppose we'll have to eat the cake ourselves," sighed Ma, but we'd forgotten the front door, which none of us ever used. The Reverend Twilling and his wife, having picked their way through the sprung milkweeds along the path, had been ringing the doorbell. It had been disconnected for years.

The Reverend, to my surprise, exhibited neither puritanical severity nor the jovial curate's hearty bonhomie. Small and fair, with wire-rimmed glasses and a neat, pointed beard, he might but for his collar have been a pharmacist or a bank teller. His wife was a hollow-boned bird whose hair, wound tight at the back of her head, seemed heavier than the rest of her. She carried a red-faced, mewling infant in a blue sleepsuit. Three weeks old, she told my mother, who bent over it with a soft "Oh," as if it had knocked the breath out of her. The baby's mother, through an act of the most vigorous self-discipline, was able to lift her eyes from its face—she smiled and shook my mother's hand. She had brought us a yellow rose, by way of welcome. It was full open, its ruffled petals flushed with pink.

"Thank you," I said. Ma had prodded me from behind to accept it. "It looks just like a ripe peach."

I was overwhelmed by my cleverness, though the adults hadn't seemed to hear me. There could be no question that this rose had a peach's glowing soul. I touched Ma's skirt to gain her attention, and she absently patted my head.

"What a lovely secluded spot you've found," Mrs. Twilling said, peering through the front window, which since it was cut through the thick stone wall admitted only the narrowest shaft of sun.

"The house of Usher!" said Ma with grim glee. My father,

when we were house-hunting, had overruled her interest in a sunny cottage closer to town. But once planted, though she never forgave him, she rooted herself as if this were her own native soil. "The house of the seven gables!" she said.

Mrs. Twilling, unsure whether she was meant to offer sympathy or admiration, edged closer to her husband.

"I suppose the town takes care of the roads," he said.

"I suppose," said Ma vaguely. Then, full of energy, remembering her role: "Sit! Sit down! What can I get you? We have sherry, port . . ."

"Tea would be nice, I think," said the Reverend, sitting, hitching his corduroy pants at the knee. His wife sat too, smoothing her skirt, her hair, then, by rote, the baby's downy skull. Her face was still and pleasant. She measured out a decorous smile. The ordinary being almost unknown to me, she seemed exotic as a gazelle. I fell in love with her.

"Katie, you make conversation," Ma said, escaping into the kitchen. "I'll make the tea."

Side by side on the sofa, our guests looked like runaways in a bus station, lost and small. Sitting cross-legged on the carpet before them, I could have reached out to trace the curve of Mrs. Twilling's ankle as it disappeared into her modest shoe. She glanced at her husband, who glanced at his watch. In the kitchen my mother, who had studied the Great Works only to be faced with guests out of—well, no author would have them!—dropped something and swore a quiet oath.

Mrs. Twilling bent toward me. Her pallor, her pointed chin and nose, her round eyes which expressed almost nothing, mesmerized me. What was she thinking? Her small, precise lips parted. I saw her small, even teeth.

"Do you go to nursery school?"

I shook my head. Ma didn't believe in nursery school and made an awful mimicry of the teacher who thought reading bad for the eyes. Now I imagined children eating cupcakes, playing croquet (with mallets, not flamingos), or making conversation, something I had just discovered myself unable to do. The phrases, even the tones we had rehearsed were wrong, too sharp, too emphatic. Nothing I could think of was polite enough anymore.

"Well," said Mrs. Twilling, whose smile had tightened somewhat at the news of my truancy. "You might like to come to Sunday school one week."

I knew this was an offer of expiation. "I'm sure that would be lovely" might have been the thing to say. I nodded. *Where was my mother?* As the silence lengthened, I felt I must repay it with something proportionately philosophical, funny, or wise, but I was mute, perhaps even invisible, and Mrs. Twilling lifted her eyes from me.

"What does *he* do?" she asked the Reverend in undertone.

He glanced toward the kitchen, but there was no sign of Ma.

"Trust fund," he said. "Invests in . . . this and that."

She nodded with the disdain I was sure she must be right to feel. It was we, I now realized, who were the strange ones, the ones always in the wrong. I racked my brain for a topic that would prove I was one of them. I decided to ask the baby's name. I would speak clearly, as Ma had taught me, and look my listener straight in the eye.

I did. His name was Adam. His mother lifted him so I could adore him more completely. His head lolled from his soft neck (a dead sunflower). His lashless, browless lids unscrewed. Tiny, intent eyes, red-rimmed like a piglet's. I blinked. The nostrils yawned in the upturned nose . . .

"He looks just like a pig!" I said. It came as a proud revelation. It was true and it was fascinating, and I had longed to fascinate.

"What, dear?" Mrs. Twilling asked, though I was sure my voice had been admirably clear. Ma was at the door with the silver tray, the pale teacups above it, the silver bowl with its hill of sugar and filigree spoon. Instead of cake, there was a plate of store cookies.

"I said," I said proudly—all eyes were on me now—"that the baby looks just like a pig. Look . . ."

"*Katie*," Ma said, grave, so beautifully grave that I knew that, though I had betrayed her in my heart a moment ago, I was delighting her now.

She blamed *Alice in Wonderland*. She never blamed me. The Twillings, not having expected my comment, could not quite take it in, so we didn't even have to apologize. Ma asked about the new parish hall and the Aid to Africa, but really she was only waiting until they left and it would be just the two of us again.

"He *did* look like a pig," she said. "*Exactly*. In fact, she looked a little like a pig herself, just around the eyes."

I felt a terrible pang then, as if the door to a whole world had been shut against me. I would never see Mrs. Twilling again, never learn anything more about her, how she might receive her guests (there must be many), or what books she might read to her son. Strange and wonderful as common life would always seem, my love for it was doomed. I had come to it too late, from too far, and I would never quite speak its language—I was bound to be Ma's ally now.

She was laughing and laughing, helplessly, rocking me against her with titanic pride. "*You*," she said, "are the most dreadful child I have ever, ever known." The cake lay where she had dropped it, in a billow of whipped cream on the floor. I pressed my face into the soft wool of her shoulder, smelled her sweet perfume.

"Wicked, wicked, wicked," she said. "Wicked to the bone."

The Honored Guest

He was one of the great character actors of the forties—played in all the big hits, brought down the house at the Belasco opening night of . . .

"You don't know the Belasco?" my mother said, seeing me foggy. "And you call yourself a theatrical publicist?"

I didn't call myself anything. I was fifteen, she was paying me ten dollars a press release, and I tried to cause her no shame. I was a fascinated fly on the wall at the theater, watching, watching, surprised now to find they could see me too.

"He went to Hollywood and was nominated for an Academy Award for the role of . . . for his performance in *Sword of Honor*" (I took an obedient note), "but didn't *win* until . . ."

"Cameron Spencer won an Oscar? Are you sure?"

She shot me that furious, wounded look: Why does no one ever believe her? "Yes, I am sure."

Al Davis, the theater's owner, shook his head. Al was a dry, wary man, celebrated in our group for the very mystery of his reserve. He played the piano at cast parties, plunging heart and both elbows into his rendition of "You Must Have Been a Beautiful Baby," grinning around his cigar. He was otherwise impervious to our enthusiasms. Our principal actress, his wife, was goaded to ever greater heights of hyperbole, hoping to engage him: no sorrow of Maura's might remain less than tragic; all her pleasures were sublime. She and my mother were much alike, so naturally suspicious: Maura took my part now and suggested Ma call the library.

Ma looked daggers at me. Here she was, finally in charge, and in front of her new employers I undermined her. "Just write," she said. "This is publicity, not private investigation."

"I want to be accurate," I said, from spite.

"Accurate!" said my mother. "This is the theater!" She spread her arms to encompass our enterprise, represented by the four of us in the one-window cabin we used as an office, our desk covered with photos of glossy ingénues, our framed playbills, our gallon of gin. We were no two-bit summer stock company, we were a two-bit *Equity* summer stock company. As we rushed to mount a new play each week, the blondes murmuring their lines to themselves over dinner as the costumer fitted a final sleeve, all of us up painting plywood for marble at dawn, it was hard to remember that the affairs of the Brimfield Playhouse were not crucial, that we were not the most important people in the world.

"He really was superb in *Sword of Honor*," Maura mused, exactly as if directed to muse, so that we could all feel how very superb he had been, how deeply he had affected her. Her voice was trained in this husky resonance, her laugh to its ascending chimes. Maura's husband, who had built the theater to woo her up from New York, no longer suffered her gladly.

"A hack," he said, "but a hack resplendent." He cut a wedge from his cigar tip and smiled a small, confidential smile at me. Only he and I dared call things by their right names. Cameron Spencer was a distant acquaintance of his, but it was Ma who had persuaded him to do us this favor, put us on the map.

"He *deserved* an Academy Award," Maura said, "whether or not he got one."

"There," said my mother. "Write it down."

"*I'll* call the library," Maura said. Handsome and dauntless as a figurehead, she lifted her hair back and smiled into the phone.

"Hello, this is Maura Fairchild Davis, at the Playhouse? Our guest star, Cameron Spencer, arrives this next week, and we were wondering if you could check for us, on what year he won the Oscar." The librarian, mundane creature, would be grateful for even this small brush with the glittering world we touched every day.

"He was *the* great character actor of the forties, you know," Maura confided. "Do you remember *Sword of Honor?*" She sighed. "He really was superb . . ."

Her smile faded, and a fine blush spread over her throat, into her cheeks. "I see," she said. "I beg your pardon. Please excuse us. Oh, dear."

"Mopping her floor," Maura said to us, in bright bewilderment. "A wrong number. She said she'd like to be of service, but she was mopping her floor."

My mother laughed herself to tears, taking us all down with her. "These things don't happen to other people, I'm sure," she said. "Why, *why* is it always us?" Even Al smiled, just to be among us. Pleasure was cheap for me then: the sound of ice rattling in a glass promised the subtlest terrors, to laugh with Al was like laughing with the gods. Cameron Spencer was coming! Outside our cavern, the theater, a rebuilt barn, stood amid thick hayfields. Hammers rang. The air was fresh with the smell of paint.

"Should I try again?" Maura asked.

"No! Nineteen forty-eight, just write it down," Ma said. "*Go ahead*, Katerina, write it down and then run up to the corner and get us a couple of limes."

Katerina. A queen's name. I'd never lived up to it, shrank beneath, in fact, the name my mother had given me during one of her many excursions into excess, the moment of triumph when I, her first child, was born. Triumph had not come often enough to her: awaiting it she had raised us good and thoughtful among the treacherous rose trellises of Republican Brimfield, had organized first the Congregational Churchwomen, then the PTA, then the tiny, furious Democratic Committee and the vigil against the war—all the while concealing my father's financial reverses and suffering, in the privacy of our sunny farmhouse, the alternate agonies of migraine and inchoate, despairing rage. She wanted to stand like the Statue of Liberty over some great harbor, but she was stuck in Brimfield, washing my father's shirts, rinsing them, wringing them, closing the faucet so hard the handle came off in her hand.

Now that Al had asked her to manage the theater, she would succeed at last, if only I would stop doubting and love her as she loved me, if I would step into the place my name had reserved for me, and shine. It was because of me, she said, that Al wanted her: his son was in my class at school, so Al had seen my honors speech and called Ma the next week. I was her talisman, the proof of her powers, and I must always stand at her side.

On the opening night of *Bring Down the Moon*, written by Arthur Winograd and starring Cameron Spencer, I wore a black dress chosen by the costumer to set my skin "Grecian white." He wrapped my shawl to show a shoulder and tucked, as I twirled for him, a silk rose into my hair. I seemed quite nearly my proper self, for the first time.

"*You look magnificent*," Ma said, emphasizing each word, as if she were sending me into battle. She lifted her white silk skirt to step onto the front terrace, her nearsighted squint making her seem languorous, half-intoxicated with the evening, the laughter of her guests, the name Cameron Spencer on her marquee.

"Is the tape showing?" she whispered. (Her dress was backless and she'd had to use masking tape in place of a bra.) I shook my head. So she tossed her head in the joy of conspiracy and went among the townswomen she despised, smiling, shaking every hand. This was hers, all hers, who had been cutting my dresses down for my sister while these ladies partook of their mountains of little sandwiches, their oceans of tea.

I, Katerina, let myself out of the box office and went around to the deck, where the last scraps of wood and muslin lay, abandoned in the haste to finish the final preparations inside. The sun burned low in a hazy sky. A dog barked, and from the dressing rooms came loud laughter, the affected jocularity of actors wound tight, ready to go on. Then an ominous rumble: someone was testing the thundersheet. The sacraments of evening. Safe above the fray, alone for a last moment, I stood as open and grateful as in a cathedral: in this green world, already blessed, we had made another of colored light and papier-mâché. It seemed as if my knowing this, my solitary contemplation, put me deeper at the center than Ma with her guests, or even Maura on stage.

"Fifteen minutes," the stage manager said, knocking at each door, purposeful and nonchalant. "Fifteen minutes, Miss Fairchild. Fifteen minutes, Mr. Spencer. Mr. Spencer? Damn, where is the old boy?"

Cameron Spencer had seemed, disappointingly, to be a perfectly ordinary aging gentleman, distant, retiring early to the special room we had reserved for him at the Brimfield Inn, never really a part of the group. He had absorbed from his various roles the manner of a lord, as lords are depicted in theater: he was courteous and aloof and one always expected to hear he was out with the hounds. Now, as my mother in her silver sandals ran along the torchlit path to find me, I realized that I had lost him, that just before she said I looked magnificent she had sent me up to bring him down from the Inn.

"I'm sorry," I said automatically, but she wasn't angry. She simply would not allow an emergency, now.

"Go up there and find him," she said, "and *run*. He's in the first scene."

It was a block uphill to the clock tower and two more around the town green to the Inn, but I found him before that, on the porch of the Methodist parsonage, watching the day go down.

"Hello, dear," he said, as I came up the steps to him. "I would stand, but . . ." But he was too drunk to stand without aid.

"We have to go to the theater," I said in a very small voice. I could hardly believe Cameron Spencer would hear me across the gulf of stature and age.

"Our car will arrive," he said, patting my wrist, ruminative, worldly-wise. Youth is always impatient. He leaned back and closed his eyes.

"It's ten minutes to curtain." This roused him. I was sorry, as I steadied him along the main street, that I had to leave his bottle beneath the wicker rocker of the sternest censor in town, but I knew Ma would be pleased.

At 8:30 the stage manager gave our honored guest a shower. At 8:40, ten minutes past curtain time, Al pushed my mother on stage to speak.

"Good evening, and welcome to the Brimfield Playhouse. Tonight we are proud to welcome a very special guest, Cameron Spencer, the greatest character actor of this century, Academy Award nominee for *Sword of Honor*, Academy Award *winner* . . ."

I heard her proud, shaken voice over the loudspeaker in the green room, where I was cutting Cameron Spencer's boutonniere from the ingénue's bouquet. Once I'd dispatched my press release, we had lost interest in the business of the Oscars, and I was curious to hear what she would say.

". . . for *Ship of the Desert*, in 1948." She had invented it. On she sailed.

At 8:50 the curtains parted to reveal the star himself, natty among the plastic vines we had trained over the arbor and sprayed with false dust. He faced his audience with perfect haughty irritation:

"Open the window, Vera. There's not a breath of air in here."

It was the first line of the third act. Maura, in chiffon peignoir with rose shears, smiled helplessly. "It has that feel, doesn't it," she said, "but you mustn't be so gloomy. Winona's giving us breakfast in the garden." She touched the paper roses. *Garden.*

"Quite," said Cameron Spencer.

Maura looked desperately about. "And you're looking forward to seeing *Teddy*, I'm sure."

With this, Cameron Spencer remembered Teddy's cue, and a flustered young man in panama hat entered stage left.

"Teddy, darling," Maura said.

We watched from the back of the theater, under the spotlight platform.

"Thank God Art Winograd is dead," Al said. He let the lobby door slam as he left, and Ma let her composure go.

"The one good thing that ever happened to me," she said, "and *look.*" Maura was fitting each line Cameron Spencer spoke like a jigsaw piece into the puzzle of the play. Again, I guessed Ma blamed me. She followed Al.

"Doesn't have Winograd's usual clarity," a man in the back row whispered to his wife. "Is it a later work?"

It was our best night ever: 235 seats sold. Back in the cabin, while the play ran its rudderless course, we counted out the box office, laying the ticket stubs out over a card table and tallying them with the cash. Al's cigar glowed in the thirty-watt gloom. We had nearly a thousand dollars, enough to pay half our past-due bills, though I'd still have to wait for my ten.

"He's done his job," Al said, grim.

Ma watched him, a smile of recognition forming, as if she were learning an essential truth. "Perfectly," she said. Satisfied, she zipped the money into the bank bag and finished her drink. "In truth," she said, "it's Katerina who's done *her* job."

First I thought this was sarcasm, but I remembered *The Beacon* had run my press release on the front page. "Where would I be without you?" Ma said, worshipful, nearly, as if she were in the play.

"Theater's such a messy art," said Al.

Out in the parking lot, a car started and drove away. But most of the audience stayed. They had come to see the star, and by the third act Cameron Spencer was sober, if drained. He ordered Maura to open the window again, and as they were now enclosed among velvet armchairs borrowed from Brimfield's finest homes, we could all appreciate his need. He had to be prompted, but he spoke always simply, from the purest feeling, as we rarely do in life. One knew his character, finally, better than any uncle in his hopes and fears, his proud folly. With the last line, wry, ironic, wise, the entire ragged play was drawn together and presented whole and sweet. A hush fell over the house. The ovation might have shaken the mice down from the rafters.

Under the spotlight platform we clapped till our hands were sore, enriching the applause, while Maura bowed deep to the stage. I unlocked the box office to bring out the red roses we had for our star. Ma was laughing again, buoyantly self-assured. She had waited for this, all those lost days at home, and never patiently: now she would accept her laurels, even if they were theater laurels fashioned of tissue and wire. She turned to me, her chronicler.

"I told you I'd do it," she said, and for a moment the vessel of her pride tipped to fill me too. Applause will cure everything, all sorrows and doubts, for as long as it lasts. I thought she might send me up with the roses—I even wanted to go.

"Once more, dear friends, into the breach," she said, turning to bear her burden of roses toward the stage.

Cameron Spencer accepted them as a man does who has received many a public bouquet. As if he *had* won the Academy Award. As if this gift, this call to the theater, were God-given, not his to claim. Spent, mortal again, he made a last, sweeping bow while my mother stepped to the edge of the spotlight, beaming as if she had made him of whole cloth and according to her own design.

Al's smile was ghostly: his teeth were small and stained and widely spaced, and in the dark at the back of the theater it seemed to be the smile of someone who saw almost all. I pulled the shawl tight around my shoulders and leaned beside him, considering triumph, smiling too. We would smile together again after the show, when my mother, called to explain *Ship of the Desert*, waved a hand and let her laugh float away like a child's balloon.

In the Zoot Car

The night before my sixteenth birthday, my sister Audie filled my mother's car with flowers she had stolen from every garden in town. Brilliant peonies, lilacs of every shade, the year's first opening roses overflowed the back seat, blocking the rear window, spilling to the ground when we opened the doors. Ma didn't care. The townspeople didn't like her, and if Audie wanted to run through their gardens in twilight, scissors flashing as the blossoms fell into her arms, Ma wouldn't stop her. She smiled and raised her eyebrows to me. After all it wasn't her fault— she hadn't told Audie to go. Now her little white car was full of pinks and lavenders and blues, and we gathered them in triumph, overwhelmed by fragrance and humidity.

"I'll swoon," I said, thinking that to swoon would be to allow the flowers their full impression, meaning to entertain my mother.

She laughed. "Swoon later," she told me. "Help me carry them inside first." It didn't matter where they came from or who they were for; my mother owned them now. She was generous, as ever: "Go look at yourself in the mirror with all those lilacs in your arms," she said to me. "You look like a painting."

We spent all day cutting them, arranging them in crystal vases and milk bottles, even filling the sink in the guest bathroom with them, since we had no guests. I had other presents:

flowered stationery, a silvery-green straw hat—a bowler—with a green ribbon, a book of plays, a printed cotton skirt, and a V-neck leotard. Pop was taking me, next week, for my driver's test. He wanted Audie to take the flowers back to the gardeners who'd grown them.

"Don't be so stuffy, Gil," Ma said. "They won't even notice the flowers are gone."

"We have the same flowers here," Pop said. "The lilacs are choking the front path." He looked from one to the other of us as if we represented some baffling and dangerous tribe, but he and Ma were past quarreling, so he said no more and left us to ourselves.

Audie's hair was cut so straight across the bottom, it looked like a blond broom. She poked a red rose into the center of one vase and straightened up, smiling.

Ma kissed the top of her head. "You're lucky they didn't come after you with shotguns," she said.

By afternoon we did have a guest. The car came carefully up the driveway, seeming to float slightly on its wheels. It was the same colors as a fancy wing-tip shoe, something from the forties. A zoot car.

"Is that Cappy?" Ma cranked open one of the upstairs windows and leaned out. "Gil, it's my brother. Kids, your uncle Cappy's here." She pulled one white bloom from a vase and tucked it in her hair on the way down the stairs. I was behind her, in new clothes, new perfume. No flower would stay in my hair.

Cap's voice was enormous. "Where's the birthday girl?" he asked, embracing my mother, as Audie, grinning, waited her turn.

I climbed over the porch railing into the garden.

"There she is!" Cappy said. "There's my princess. She's growing up pretty, she's going to be as pretty as her ma."

The car was mine. Uncle Cap gave me the keys and showed

me all the buttons, to open the windows and the trunk, to move the radio antenna up and down. The seats were beige leather, the top beige linen, the paint metallic brown. It was a Lincoln Continental, eight years old, as wide and square as a river barge. I stood in the driveway with the keys in my hand, beyond disbelief. It might as well have been a rocket.

"She can't keep a gift like this," Pop said. "It's too much. This is absurd." Cappy had gone in to call a taxi to take the train home.

"He wants her to have it. He'll be terribly disappointed if you don't let her keep it."

"It's some kind of illegal payoff, you know that."

"Well, Katie didn't do anything wrong. Don't punish *her* for it."

They stood on the porch, hushed, but arguing. At the sound of a door slamming inside, Ma dropped her hands from her hips and came over to me.

"Now, be sure to thank him, honey," she said, pushing my hair back from my face. "It's a beautiful car."

Theater, that's my mother's business. Pinstripe patent-leather Lincoln Continentals might rain from heaven and she would be graciously, nonchalantly thankful for each. Her dresses were handed down from her sister or borrowed from the costume shop, but though they pulled at the shoulders or had to be draped to hide a stain, they could not shade her beauty. She had only to throw her head back, laughing, and the men in a room would gather around her, talking politics, psychology, theater, touching her shoulder, puffed with opinion and booming with their own jests.

Cappy called to her from the porch, "You can drive it too, Lila Ann, if Kate will let you." He handed the registration to my father as he came down. "It's in your name, Gil . . ."

"Cappy, we can't let you do this." Pop started off strong. He was right. The car seemed a burden to me, as if I would have to carry it. "It's too much, we can't accept it."

"It's registered to you, kiddo; if you don't want to let her drive it, that's fine." Cappy kissed me, over my ear, through my hair. "My princess deserves a proper chariot," he said.

Until I got my license, I was allowed to drive the car only between the house and the corner, half a mile. We had to go to New York on Saturday, though, Ma had a meeting, and she was taking Audie and me to see Grandma while she was there. It was the first really hot day that year—the lilacs were drooping from their branches. Audie and I sat at the kitchen table in city clothes, eating breakfast.

"I'm going to stop off and see Jack Cirillo on the way home," Ma said.

Pop was buttering toast. He looked up at her, over his glasses. "Why?"

"I have to talk to him. He's producing . . . theater stuff. I have to talk to him about the playhouse." Ma was wearing white linen, a career-girl dress. Laugh lines, or squint lines, fanned out from her eyes. She looked steadily at Pop, and he looked away. I, too, wondered why she wanted to see Jack Cirillo, and Audie glanced across at me with raised eyebrows.

"I need the car later," Pop said. "I'm going to buy lawn seed."

"We'll take the Lincoln."

Quietly Pop said, "I will not have you driving my daughters to New York in a car that may or may not lose its brakes, or its steering, or its headlights at any time."

"Katie," Ma said, "are you afraid to ride in your car? Audie, are you afraid of the car?"

"Of course not," Audie said. "I could probably fix the car if anything broke." On her arm Audie wore a water-transfer tattoo of some fake motorcycle gang. Her dress was blue, with long ribbons tied at the neck and little shiny buttons all the way down the front.

"I don't care," I said, "but if we take the VW, you won't be able to get your seed."

"I *wish* you'd pull your hair off your face, at least when you're in the kitchen," Ma said to me.

I slunk away, with Audie in tow, out through the living room to the front window. In the driveway my zoot car glistened.

"Lila." My father's voice came from the kitchen. "You know your brother, and you know that car is in some way illegal, possibly dangerous. Will you at least wait until I've had a chance to check on it before you cross the state line?"

"Don't be so melodramatic. Do you think they'll slap me in leg-irons and haul me off to prison?" She was laughing, and her voice softened so much, I couldn't hear the rest. She came through the living room and ran lightly up the stairs. Out the window, behind her, I could see Pop going up the hill in back of the house, shaking his head.

We were exactly a mile from home (I could see on the special odometer for trips) when Ma pulled over and asked if Cappy had shown me how to put the top down. Audie leaned over the seat to watch as I worked the little chrome lever that opened the trunk, as the roof folded over our heads and the trunk ground shut on it. The exposed sky was brilliant, the sun hot on my shoulders. We set off again, laughing, shouting to each other over the wind, waving to everyone: other cars, ladies pushing oversize lawn mowers, people in wedding regalia outside a church. Ma drove very slowly—she said she was frightened of traffic. We missed nothing all the way to New York, and nothing missed us. By the time we got there it was too late for a visit to Grandma's. Ma double-parked and left us to guard the car.

"They won't tow my children away," she said.

While she was gone, we planned what to do if, indeed, they

would tow her children away. Should we scramble out in different directions, run between buildings, and leave the car to its fate? Pretend to be immigrants and not know that double-parking was illegal in America? We practiced speaking in tongues. Audie said we should play Lorelei—we combed our hair and hoped policemen would be so moved by our beauty they would overlook the car. No policeman came. The buildings were so high they seemed to taper together above the narrow street.

A huge truck pulled up behind us. I could see the driver lift his arm and jerk his elbow down to pull the horn, but it startled me anyway. Surely, every cop in New York had heard it. I tried to explain to the driver, in sign language, that I didn't have my license yet and could ruin my life by trying to move the car. The endless horn sounded like a steamship, roaring toward us between the buildings. Audie and I, dwarfed by the noise, watched each other over the seat. If my mother heard it from the tenth floor, I'm sure she didn't look out to find the source. Finally, as if we were some kind of obstruction that the usual methods had failed to dissolve, the driver climbed down from the cab and approached us. He was sturdy but not as tall as I had expected, and not much older than we were. Audie and I could handle him, I thought.

"Who put this thing here?" he asked me.

"My mother," Audie said. He couldn't berate her mother. He looked at us, and I looked at us, too. At fourteen and sixteen, we were only slightly fleshed. Audie had biceps from basketball, I had breasts. Our hair was brushed one hundred times a day, outside and in. Mine hung over most of my face. I wore my new leotard and my new skirt, my knees protruding sharply from underneath, and I wanted to put my hat on so much that my hands trembled in its direction as if they were not in my control.

"Can either of you drive?" he asked.

"I can," I said.

23

He seemed doubtful. "Do you have the keys?"

I did. "This is my car," I told him, and I glanced up to see if he was surprised that a woman as young as myself should possess a wing-tip car, but he simply put both hands on the door and swung over it and into the front seat.

"We can't go very far," I said, handing him the keys. "My mother'll be out any minute."

He looked at me. "I don't want to go anywhere in *this*," he said. "I just want to get it out of the way."

Ma came running out through the revolving door. She stopped, seeing the truck and the car, and gave me a wide, deceiving smile before she went around to the driver's side.

"Oh dear, am I in the way? I'm awfully sorry. I have a terrible time understanding the parking in New York. It's so nice of you to move the car for me, but we're about to go, so we'll just get it out of your way."

The man was staring at the pedals, and as my mother prattled over his bowed head, he began to look insubstantial.

"I'm Lila Vanderwald," Ma was saying, "and these are my daughters, Kate and Audie." She smiled, and her hair brushed across her shoulder as she leaned down to shake his hand.

"Ronnie Garkofsky," he said, clearing his throat. "This street is too narrow. I've got some kind of problem on this street every week. Sometimes I get two wheels up on the sidewalk and just drive through."

Audie laughed. "I'll bet they get out of the way then."

"You should see it." He grinned. "Even in New York, people move for an eighteen-wheeler."

There were horns behind the trunk now, all the way to the end of the block. The sun was shining straight down between the buildings, and the noise was rising toward it like a tide.

Ronnie Garkofsky got out of the car, shook Ma's hand, and ran back to his truck. Ma started the Lincoln.

"I'm gone twenty minutes and you're all ready to run off with a perfect stranger," she said.

Audie turned around, lifted her arm in the air, and made a yanking motion, as if pulling an overhead horn. Ronnie pulled. His horn cut through the little hoots and bleeps of the cars behind us and seemed to send us forward along the street. He pulled it once more before he turned, and we didn't see him again.

On the way to Jack Cirillo's we practiced our new sign language. Ma drove so slowly that all the trucks had to pass us, and as they did we yanked furiously at the air. They honked. There was not one exception. Enormous men honked twice and waved sausagelike arms at us; scrawny men with few teeth blew long bugle sounds; handsome mustached men like the men in cigarette commercials honked quickly and swooped around us and away. The honking carried us along the parkway while Audie perched on the seat back and waved like a politician in a parade. My hat shimmered beside me, my hair flew, New York blew by and out to sea on a chorus of truck horns, and we waved to Yonkers, and Westchester, and Valhalla, where graves stretched for miles, until we crossed into Connecticut and everything became perfect green. Jack Cirillo lived on Long Island Sound. Well before we arrived we could see the water, always appearing and receding, more a swamp than a sea. He had a dock and a boat, Ma said, so his children could explore the salt marshes when they visited. And a family of swans lived on the water in back of the house.

Jack Cirillo, when he came out to meet us, walked casually, spoke slowly and deeply, as if he had a pleasant, private idea beneath everything he said. Ma had been combing her hair, and passed me the comb under her hand. I arranged my hat, and she pushed my hair back beneath it, off my face. Jack Cirillo kissed Ma's mouth, but quickly, and Audie glanced at me for confirmation. I didn't care if Ma was having an affair with him; in fact I hoped it was true. I liked the way his watchband gripped his wrist; I liked the dark hair curling at the opening of his shirt. He shook Audie's hand and patted her head, admiring her tattoo, and when he shook my hand, he kissed me lightly, beside my eye.

"This is too much," he said to my mother. "God knows what people are going to think I'm keeping over here. You've got a built-in entourage."

Ma smiled, lifting her chin.

"And you deserve one," he added.

We went directly to the backyard, where Jack Cirillo brought out two pitchers of lemonade, a green plastic one for us and a smaller glass one, which he set down by the chairs at a distant corner of the lawn. A bottle of gin already rested on one of the chairs.

"Jack and I have to talk about the theater," Ma said. "You girls can explore, but don't leave the property, and don't bother us. We need to concentrate." He poured out drinks and they sat down.

The dock was a beam jammed into the bank, and the boat was only a rowboat, but the swans were wonderful. They drifted like lilies along the surface of the water, luminous and imposing. If I could touch them, I thought, I would find them soft but resilient, like giant meringues. Audie took off her shoes and climbed into the rowboat. Every time she stretched her arm out toward the swans, the ribbons that were meant to tie the neck of her dress trailed farther into the water.

"Let's row out to them," she said.

"We don't have oars. We have to stay at the dock," I told her.

"Well, let's pretend we're rowing. Come on, Kate, you sit on the front seat. Look," she said to me as I tried to keep my balance and my hat, stepping into the boat, "they're putting on a show for us."

The swans were weaving patterns around one another, bobbing just beyond our reach as we cooed and kissed at them and splashed water to catch the rainbows in it. We tossed them knotted grasses, which they refused even to examine. I wrapped one of Audie's sodden ribbons around my neck, but it didn't keep me cool for long. I could feel myself losing my will against the sun, and I stretched over the edge of the boat and arched my back up into its warmth. Audie was quiet, staring abstractedly across the water. On land my mother's legs were drawn up beneath her; with one arm around them she rested her head against the chair and laughed. Two things sparkled: the gin he poured into her glass, and her eyeglasses, dangling from her left hand, unused.

"I'm so hot I think I'm going to melt," I said. "I'm *so* glad I'm not all covered with feathers."

"*They're* comfortable," Audie said. "They're half in the water. If you want to cool off, you should just dip your head in."

I did. I leaned far over the side, watching my hair fan out along the water as I lowered my face. The water was stunningly cold, and when I had wrung my hair nearly dry, I forced it down my collar, where it would cool my blood with every pulse.

"Now your hair's going to dry all frizzy," Audie said. "I'm exhausted. How much longer are they going to talk?"

"I don't know. I'm starving."

"Look, the swans are swimming out to sea." Audie pointed to them receding against the low, green water. "They're too fragile! They'll break up on the waves. Come back, come back!" she called to them. "Maybe we could feed them."

She got out and ran up the lawn. Jack Cirillo had left a plate of crackers on the picnic table for us. Neither he nor my mother turned to look as Audie ran back to the boat.

"Be careful," I told her. "They bite."

The idea was ludicrous; it would be like dancers stepping off the stage to pinch their audience. The swans drifted guilelessly beyond her reach. But Audie reached farther, balancing her way out to the end of the dock and scattering broken crackers in front of her. They noticed. It was the first reaction I had seen. The smallest swan circled and returned, bending its head to the water, coming up beneath the cracker, swallowing it in a single gulp. Audie laughed. "Look, it loves my crackers!" She held one out and the swan came toward her, stretching its neck. The two others followed.

"They like me," Audie said. "These crackers are good."

She ran back along the dock to the edge of the water. "Come here, little swan," she called.

As the swan floated toward the upheld cracker, I could see it was not little at all: in fact it was nearly the size of a large wedding cake. It gave the appearance of nonchalance, drifting as if the current had shifted in our direction. The older swans followed it. I was envious of Audie, who could persuade reasonless creatures to come to her. The little one straightened its neck, lifting its head to her hand. I leaned back against the rim of the boat. Under the arc of Audie's outstretched arm I could see my mother nod her head, making a point.

"Look," Audie said, "the mother wants a cracker too!"

The largest of the swans had zoomed into position under her arm, pushing the baby away. I was amazed at its sudden energy. It reached up to Audie's hand.

"Kate, look!" she called, but the creature ignored the cracker altogether and bit her. The cracker fell. Audie yelped and pushed back from the water and the swan, but the malevolent creature was on the shore in a second, squawking as if Audie had bitten it. Ma was on her feet, I was on my feet, rocking the boat, and Audie—poor Audie—was running as awkwardly and as fast as the pursuing swan. It seemed a real bird now, a giant chicken.

"Just run straight up the lawn!" Ma shouted. Audie did, and the swan followed her as far as some invisible human boundary, turned, and stumbled back to the water. My mother, like a mother swan, took Audie in. Jack Cirillo seemed suddenly out of place. He poured a glass of lemonade for Audie, held it out to her, poured gin into it. I saw this as I walked up the lawn to them. Breathing loudly, tossing back the gin, Audie handed me a barrette.

"Put your hair up in this," she whispered. "It looks terrible."

"I told you they bite," I said. I tried to pull my hair into some kind of order, twisting and pinning it, drawing from my face like a curtain. "You're lucky they didn't pull you down to a watery grave," I said.

Ma was laughing softly, helplessly.

"Do they make a practice of this?" she asked Jack Cirillo. "Can you sic them on burglars?"

"I swear I've never seen it before," he said. "Usually they ignore people altogether."

"I wish I could have seen it too," Audie said. She raised her arms and collapsed lightly to the ground.

"She has a flair for comedy," Ma explained.

Jack Cirillo laughed a quiet inward laugh. He was surveying us, I thought, as if we too were a flock, similar to our motley attitudes, biting at our feathers, shifting our weight. I could feel Audie's barrette begin to slip in my hair, and Ma said that we should leave.

"But I haven't had a chance to talk to your daughters," Jack said.

"Jack, I can't stay. You know the situation. He's already furious. And now I've got this car that God only knows if it works or what. I'll bring the girls again sometime."

"Will they still be as lovely as this?"

My mother showed some surprise. She looked at each of us for a moment, almost involuntarily, and back to him, smiling. "They may be lovelier. Audie probably won't have that tattoo."

"I'll always have this tattoo," Audie said. "I'm gonna have this *really* tattooed on both my arms."

"*And*," Ma said, "Kate will have a different hairdo. She will have given up the Irish-washerwoman look."

I was stricken. I had expected the barrette to please her. Jack Cirillo extended his hand and tucked a loose strand of my hair back, running his finger slowly behind my ear.

"I like this look," he said. "It was very popular when I was in France." He watched me with such intensity, I could not believe he was really seeing me, and his hand returned to my head. "Remove one pin and her hair will be all over the pillow, they used to say."

No one spoke. The swans were back on the water, gliding peacefully past one another. The sun was still hot, hot, and I stood in the heavy air under the light press of Jack Cirillo's hand.

"Jack," my mother said finally, half angrily, "you are absolutely impossible." Her own smile seemed slowed by the sun.

In the car, my mother seemed older to me. Audie raised her arm, signaling a truck driver to honk, but Ma said the noise was giving her a headache. I smoothed my hands down over the front of my dress and stretched my arms out. From the back of my hair I pulled the one pin. My new green straw hat lay beside me. I arranged it on my head.

"You're going to lose that hat," Ma said.

"It fits me perfectly," I told her. "It's very snug on my head."

She was driving faster than usual, perhaps anxious to get home to my father's wrath. In the back, Audie was quiet, even subdued; she rested her head against the seat, her skin reddening in the wind. Across the dividing strip of lawn, a very few cars headed toward New York against the sun. Connecticut was an expanse of lawn and low trees, hazy and leafy, the light so strong at this slant that I felt its impression surely as if it were a hand on my shoulder. I suppose it seemed that such a force would also keep my hat on in the wind, but at the first curve I felt it lift off my head. I wasn't immediately regretful; as I saw it roll away, its silvery-green straw in the brighter green at the edge of the road, I thought, "Now I know why they call it a bowler."

Audie yelled, "Katie, your hat!"

"Ma, my hat's gone!" For the first time I wondered if she could hear me over the wind. "It blew away." How blessed were the drivers across the highway, speeding toward my hat! I felt I would cry.

"We can't get back there," Ma said. Her voice rose in annoyance. "I *told* you to take it off," she said. "It's ten miles to the turnoff, and we couldn't just stop on the highway, even if we did find it. It's probably already been run over anyway." Now I thought she would cry. "*Why* did you have to wear it, all of a sudden? Nobody can see you now."

"It's your own fault, Katie," Audie said.

"Well, don't make her feel any worse about it," Ma said.

I couldn't have felt any worse about it. I knew how childish it would be to cry over a lost hat, so I closed my eyes and tried to forget it. I tried to think of my new car, or of the glorious eve of my birthday, when Ma and Audie and I had felt like three goddesses in our stolen bower. Instead, I thought of Jack Cirillo, until I could remember exactly his slow voice and his slow touch and could feel my own fearful pleasure again. Ma, never a masterful driver, was creeping along in the right lane now, and car after car whipped past us, sounding like scythes. Then I heard a siren.

"I'm only going forty. They can't want *me*," my mother said. The car pulled up beside us. "My God," Ma said, "this car *is* hot."

But the policeman was smiling. "Did any of you ladies lose a hat?" he asked.

"Me!" I said. "I did." He produced it, perfectly intact. To my mother he said, "You shouldn't drive so slowly on this high-way, ma'am. It can cause an accident when you get so many vehicles built up behind you." He was plump and blue-eyed and cheerfully exasperated, as if he had spent too many days chasing cars full of deciduous women, natural outlaws, who shed their hats and scarves in the wind.

"Officer, I'm sorry," my mother said. "I'm not used to driving this car yet, and I'm afraid if I step on the gas too hard it'll just shoot out from under us. And I get so nervous driving in traffic, I just think it's better to be on the safe side. But I'll try to drive faster now, because I don't want to cause an accident."

He stepped back. "Well, it's just a suggestion," he said. "Have a nice day, now. And keep hold of that hat."

"I will," I said, and I felt my mother's smile, suddenly, on my own lips: a smile of fondness and defiance mixed, a tiny challenge. "Thank you so much," I said to the policeman. My mother stepped on the gas, and we were off like a shot.

"I'd like a pair of driving gloves," she said to me. "Brown and beige, to match the car."

"We'll each get a pair," I told her.

"I'm not sure they make them in children's sizes," Ma said.

I stretched my hands out in front of me. They were slender, strong, and against the dashboard they showed a pale, almost luminous shade of white. They were not the hands of a child, but I didn't say that to Ma. In a week I would have my driver's license. I pressed the leather of the seat; it was perfectly resil-ient, rising up against my hand. I could hear the engine shift to a higher gear, and I could feel the smoothness, the power, of the new speed. I wanted to tell someone that this was my car. I wanted to tell my mother that I *loved* my car, but I decided not to. Instead, I tucked a strand of hair slowly behind my ear.

In the back seat Audie crooked her elbow and pulled an imaginary horn, but no truck answered. There were no trucks on the highway.

"Bee-Beep," I said.

"Honk, *hooonk*," went my mother, imitating swans. "You were so funny, Audie, running from that swan." She reached back over the seat, and Audie squeezed her hand.

"We have to make a plan to cheer your father up," Ma said.

"He'll probably be happy enough to see we aren't in jail," I told her.

"He should be," Audie said. "We're incorrigible."

She was right. We turned off the highway, past the bright, defenseless gardens of Connecticut that lined the road home.

Katie Vanderwald

Where there was a pea pod, Audie saw a pea pod. She seized it, snapped it into her colander, and moved on. Lucky, or there would have been no dinner, because Kate, having picked only one pod, felt she had harvested earthly grace itself, and wasn't this enough? She was satisfied— she was grateful— as long as the dirt was black, the vines lush, and the squashes blooming in the next row.

Now they were homely peas again, a square of butter softening over them while Ma poured milk into the blue pitcher and Chucky perched on the stepstool to wash his hands. He was fair and tousled, a straw angel, but Ma turned his palms up and saw the truth.

"These may be wet," she said, making a monstrously sour face, for the benefit of the girls, "but they are *not* washed."

A baffling oracle. Chuck, his head full of beetle lore from the day outside, returned to the sink. He was the youngest, and the boy, at everyone's mercy. Sitting straight, at the head of the table, he searched for an adult topic.

"What's for dessert?" he asked.

"What do you mean, what's for dessert?" Ma said. She plucked the vase of petunias away from his notorious elbow and set it out of reach on the sill. "Do you think we're some kind of ranch-house people who think about food all the time? Pick a peach if you want dessert."

"Ma-a." The peaches were still little green fists on the tree.

"Well . . . raspberries, then, since you have the courage to eat out of those hands."

"We have dessert when Pop's home," he said.

"Then it should be clear enough," she said, "that there will be no dessert tonight."

Ma was like the weather. Her children basked or sought shelter, depending on the prevailing wind, and to mention Pop was seeding the clouds. If they were careful, though, they could bring her back to them. It was like coaxing a deer to your hand, and gentle Audie did it best.

"You sit down too, Ma," she said, patting the chair beside her. Ma wouldn't eat with them, but when Pop was away she would sit and listen to their day's adventures, her attention so perfect that every triumph was exalted and every disaster redeemed in the pleasure of telling the tale. Kate's duty (and glory) was to examine each day in all its detail and present it whole and alive, over dinner, to Ma.

They had all been good days that summer. Kate was sixteen, Audie fourteen, and since Pop had lost all the money, Ma had gone back to work and was paying her daughters to look after the house and garden, and keep an eye on Chucky, who was only six.

They ran free, within the limits of their preserve. When Pop bought the property, he had been riding the futures market like a white wave, and they could have whatever they wanted. They wanted a farm, a castle, a cave, a precipice with lake beneath, an orchard, an arbor, a swamp, and a clear stream. If you looked with a generous eye, you could see they had got it all, and without leaving Connecticut. The formal garden had grown wild among its trellises, the goldfish pond leaked, but the house was properly cavernous, built of stone from the fields where sheep now grazed. It faced south along the Wiscoponomuc Brook, in the shade of a forested hill. Chucky ruled the two tiny islands upstream from the bridge, watched by Audie from the crotch of the red maple, which held her like the palm of a giant hand.

Kate never left the house. Her chores took hours. Ironing, she felt determined as a Chinese laundress striving for the sake of the moon-faced infants who clung to her skirts while she worked. When she dusted the piano, she would sit and, though she had neglected to practice, would imagine her début: wearing a plain black sheath (to shame vanity, before art), she would swoop over the first chord like a lioness on a gazelle, and then— fluid, agile, precise, beginning with the lower, yearning registers and drawing in the upper strands one by one—she would restore the music to its living form. Later, in their bleak, cold-water flat (she pictured a sink with one faucet and a poor ragged towel), her husband would press her to him, searching her face, worried, awed. It would be wonderful to play the piano, she was sure.

Kate was noble, Audie thought, unfathomable, and embarrassing. She might look up from shelling peas, as she had done that afternoon, and say, "What if you had to leave the country, to follow the man you loved. Would you go?"

"You mean, to get married?" Audie asked, feeling squeamish, shaking the bowl to see if they had enough.

"No, I mean *love*," Kate said, with such force that Audie shrank. And giggled.

"Forget it," Kate said. "I mean things of the *soul*."

So she did. Her soul escaped in ways she herself could not hope to follow, and returned to whisper tales of things she would never see. Now, suddenly, she was having a romance, but she had learned, talking to Audie that afternoon, not to chop prodigious feeling into words.

So when Ma was sitting and ready to hear all, Kate had

nothing to say. "Well," she started, and finally turned to Audie, "did we have a good day?"

"Um," Audie said, "a pretty good day. We had a guest."

"A guest?" Ma raised an apprehensive eyebrow. The week before, a magazine salesman had found the house somehow and plagued them until Audie went back up her tree, leaving him to pace underneath. Like a frustrated hound, as Kate told it. It was her job to keep the pot boiling! Any secret worth keeping would be cruel to hoard.

"Kate's friend Amir," Audie said.

"He's a Turk," Kate explained. "Aunt Elayne brought him back from her trip."

"Quite a souvenir," Ma said. She took Kate's chop bone and sucked at the marrow. Elayne was Kate's boyfriend's aunt, a dietitian whose quest for a husband kept Ma well amused.

"He came to see the American countryside," Audie said.

"Actually," Kate said, "he came to see *me*." Ma's eyes widened, for the thickening of plot. "We went for a walk in the woods," Kate said.

She meant to stop, but their silence made her guilty. "I got a little lost," she said, "and we came to a place I never saw before. All birch trees and a soft, soft forest floor—you could imagine Indians there."

What an adventure it had been! Kate knew she was none of the things she imagined, neither delicate nor particularly receptive, and certainly not Chinese: Ma was black-Irish, Pop the palest Dane. She was a pitiful, straggly thing, with a face made mostly of glasses and teeth. When a man as lithe and insinuating as Amir wanted to touch her, it was proof of the power of dreams.

"So I said, 'I think we're lost,' and then . . . he *took* me in his arms, and *bent* me back, and kissed me and kissed me, just like Clark Gable."

"My God, Kate." The indulgent smile froze on Ma's face. "How old is this boy?"

"Twenty-five."

Audie was paying terrible attention to her peas, and Chucky said, "Lost? Only a moron could get lost up there."

Kate had sent something of herself up, kitelike, that afternoon, to meet Amir on his lofty crag, and here it crashed back at her feet and was trampled by the careless throng.

"What about Bobby?" Ma asked.

Bobby. His family was on vacation. Now that she thought of him, Kate remembered that he never washed his hair and didn't dare say he loved her, though he went for her blouse like a nursing infant every time they were alone. Nothing she did with Bobby was worthy of a report.

"He's in Hyannis," she said.

"Boy, you're tough," Ma said. "You must get it from your father."

Audie flashed a quick warning, and they waited to see if the cloud would pass.

Chucky wasn't attending. "May I have the milk, *pleeze?*" he asked. Ma turned the pitcher so he could reach the handle.

"And I'll come pick raspberries with you, okay?" Audie said, finding the thread, about to mend the conversation, but Chucky was pouring the milk over his chop.

"Chucky!"

"Oh," he said, and put the pitcher down, still in his trance, watching as a couple of peas swirled to the center of the plate. "I'm sorry," he said, "I was thinking of . . ."

"You *never* think," Ma said. "Look at that. What's the matter with you? Now you'll be hungry all night."

"I won't, Ma," he said sorrowfully. "I'll eat raspberries."

"Get up," she said. "Get out of here. We're all alone in the woods here, don't you understand? We can't just run out for a sandwich." Ma had arrived from Manhattan full of pastoral romance, but the woods loomed too dark for her, with Pop always away. She took up Chucky's plate so fast, the milk splashed over the table, onto the floor.

"Now see what you made me do?" she said.

"You rest, Ma," Audie said. "We'll do the dishes."

"GO!" Ma roared, and they faded out the back door.

Down by the brook Chuck spread skunk cabbage leaves with mud and rolled them. "These are fish," he said. "Want a bite?"

Kate put her feet in the water, and real fish darted between her ankles. Amir had kept trying her name, as he tried all English words. He could stretch the plain "Katie" until it sounded narcotic. She fell asleep that night rehearsing the memory, while Ma and Chucky laughed in the kitchen, eating peanut butter out of the jar.

Mrs. Schnippers played the double bass, and looked like a double bass, but taught the piano, which was more in demand.

"Well," she said, "I've never heard anyone play with more expression." A smile tempered her enormous face.

"And that's the hard part, really. Later you'll learn the notes. Here . . ." She slid over and went through the first few measures, then threw caution to the winds and played the whole piece.

"I see," Kate said, "I *do.*" But Mrs. Schnippers was too involved to stop.

"I was careening where Haydn meant to spin," Kate said, and Mrs. Schnippers nodded emphatically, while the music went round. Kate was sure now that she could do it too.

When she couldn't, her fingers stumbling and colliding over the keys, Mrs. Schnippers promised that practice would help. Her Saint Bernard, on the rag rug, shuddered in his sleep. Mrs. Schnippers had left the conservatory to marry Mr. Schnippers, who was out with the cows.

It was milking time, and time for the 5:35 from New York,

which, after Pop got off at Wassaic, would retreat as neatly as if reversed on film, leaving him silhouetted, briefcase in hand and coattails flying, against the pasture that sloped up behind the track. Ma, in her best white dress and her pearls (descended through Pop's family to settle around her neck), had dropped Kate at the lesson and gone to the station with Audie and Chuck. She loved to laugh in lipstick, holding Chucky transfixed, but as Pop approached, the mouth went straight. He kissed the cheek and turned to the children. "Lucky Chucky! Auderino!" Ma, who said love made him speak nonsense, would turn away. When Pop got in the driver's seat, he'd start to sneeze. Hay fever. They'd picked buckets of bee balm and loosestrife in his honor that morning, and Chuck's hands were yellow with pollen.

"Do you get any chance to play the bass now?" Pop asked Mrs. Schnippers while Kate gathered her music. The double bass leaned beside the empty music stand, which cast a scroll-work shadow on the wall.

"Oh, yes," she said. "We have our Wednesday quintet."

Pop smiled to show Kate might learn renunciation here, but he lost his easy demeanor as soon as they left the house.

"It's high summer," he said, to break the silence as they walked back to the car, looking over Don Schnippers' fields. Kate scrunched into the back seat with Audie and Chuck.

"How was the lesson?" Ma asked. Did she know? Last week, Pop had stayed in New York, so Kate had driven home from her lesson the long way, past Elayne's. Amir had been sitting on the front step alone. He looked so dangerous, with those quick eyes and long fingers! She had only sat with him an hour, trying to answer his questions about American girls while he watched her mouth form the words.

She had told Ma she was late because Mrs. Schnippers got carried away. Kate had reported wishes as horses, and molehills as the mountains of pain they caused, but she had never truly built a lie before. As soon as she had spoken, she believed herself, and Ma's suspicion seemed unfair.

"She said she'd never heard anyone play with more expression," Kate said.

"Expression," said Pop, who could launch a great distance from such a word. "That's emotion, I suppose. The emotional force. That's what music is, basically, wouldn't you say? It's true in the market too. Everyone gets the same information—it's instinct that sets one apart."

He was off, explaining how a drought might inflate corn prices while beef would plummet, or how it might work the other way around. Finance was a heady geometry to him, but Ma had had to sell their living room furniture, through a newspaper ad. She reached back over the seat and squeezed Chucky's hand.

Her doubts had poisoned the atmosphere at home, Pop said, and now he often spent weekends with his mother in New Rochelle.

Marry an orphan, Ma told them.

"I," she said, "do not need the recommendation of some teacher to be proud of my children."

Pop had lost track of the subject. "A recommendation *can* be the worst indicator," he said. "It's usually best to move against the crowd . . ."

They turned up the dirt road over Kepple Hill, where boulders tilted like ruins in the fields, with cornrows rippling outward. Everything was the dusty green-gold of August. But Kate would go to live in Amir's barren country and bend herself to his ways. And no oil-lit tents either, she admonished herself, no Arabian Nights. They'd live in a tiny apartment over an asphalt bazaar. Passion would have to suffice.

"I see what you mean, Pop," Audie said, staring out the window.

"I don't," Ma said. "I'd say expression was the force of the will, *if* I was asked. I'd say Kate should write symphonies of her own."

Operas, Kate thought, everything. What a lush world! When a flock of blackbirds scattered and regrouped overhead, she felt sure they were hearing Haydn too.

Without furniture the living room had a brute, medieval look: the beams were tree trunks again, and the fireplace was big enough to roast a foe. The piano, a concert grand that had materialized after Pop made a killing in July wheat and Ma made a breakfast of Moët & Chandon, stood alone on the blue rug as if it had set off to sea. Kate started the sonata again. Then again. And another time. This was dedication, a rational art and a noble one. She sat back to think *how* noble, and pictured a conservatory: the slim, pointed window of the practice room, the weary delirium after hours of work, toast and tea and *Lives of the Composers* back at the dorm. *This* was expression: playing the music, you could *feel* the life of the composer. You saw the women walking under his window, heard their laughter and guessed their hearts, too.

Ma had shooed them all out of the kitchen so she could talk to Pop. They had so many catastrophes! Last week the washing machine had overflowed: *back* they had stumbled as the sudsy flood advanced, bearing brassieres like bloated corpses on its crest. There had been no clean clothes, not a rag, until the girls, wrapped in tablecloths like saris, had waded into the brook and pounded the laundry on stones. They were equal to any disaster, Ma told them. She told Pop he had left them at the mercy of the tides.

"Gasket must have gone," Pop said. "I didn't realize it was that old."

"Of *course* not," Ma said. Her voice was turning, and Kate at the piano girded herself as a passenger will press an imaginary brake. "You weren't *here*."

"I can't be two places at once," he said, petulant as Chucky.

"So hide your head in mommy's apron," Ma said, "or under it."

"Don't be vulgar, Lila."

"Vulgar?" She sounded as if he'd named her place of birth. *"Why not?* Vulgar, that's what I am, vile and stinking with no clean clothes, unlike the Great Mother Vanderwald, Our Lady of the Suburbs with her ice-blue eyes and her crystal cunt."

Here was a word Kate had never heard her mother speak, and she closed the piano lid and escaped upstairs. If she were braver, she knew, she would have gone to her parents' aid. "Now you've lost track of the problem," she'd say, pulling out chairs so they could sit and listen. "The problem is she misses you, Pop. She's afraid you don't love her." She'd be very stern with him: "You cannot substitute facts for truths," she'd tell Pop. "Nobody's asking you to be in two places at once." And she would remind Ma that Pop was afraid of her and she ought to be nicer to him.

" 'Tis I," she said, vamping in the doorway of her parents' bedroom, where Audie and Chuck were watching TV, "the lovely one." She plunked herself down with them on the quilt.

"Having a little talk down there, are they?" Audie said, but as they turned their smiles together, they heard Ma coming up.

"You were delivered with ice tongs! The world's first test-tube baby, bloodless product of Vanderwald Laboratories . . ." She went past them to the mirror and tore the pins from her hair while Pop stayed at the door. "The vulgar Lila Corrigan, not worthy of the likes of you, you self-righteous-petit-bourgeois-son-of-a-bitch, with your ancestors and your—"

"Shut up," Pop said, as if desperate to stop a leak. "Just shut up," he said again, although she was silent. "It's a wonder I come here at all." The same rage that freed Ma's tongue bound his; he stood still for a moment in confusion and went back down the stairs.

"—and your pearls," she yelled after him. The diva had reached her great moment, her audience rapt, in pajamas. With one wrenching twist the pearls were everywhere, skittering along the floor, hopping in the rug.

"They're secretions, vulgar secretions, you know," she called down the stairs, and sank sobbing on the bed.

"Do you think I'm vulgar?" she asked Audie, who was hugging her, rocking her by the shoulders back and forth.

"No, Ma, I think you're beautiful" (and I think she's bananas, she'd tell Kate tomorrow).

"Me too," Chucky said, and she drew him in.

Kate rolled a pearl between her fingers. "He only said it," she said, "because you made that . . . crack . . . about Grandma." Dear God, she hadn't meant to, but she was speaking with cold rage. Ma looked up incredulous from Audie's shoulder.

"Who do you think you are?" she said. "Get out of here. You're just like the rest of them."

Kate stood, dumb, defiant.

"Get out!" Ma said. Kate went.

The keys to the VW were on a hook by the front door. On the porch swing, in the dark, Pop sat with bent head. He didn't look up when she passed.

Other times she had gone to Bobby's, to tremble in his kitchen while his hearty mother fried a steak for her cats. But seeing the lamp in his window, lit against thieves, while the family was away, she felt lonely only for a minute. Then it seemed just another slash against whatever ropes held her down on the earth, as an angry new confidence tugged her away. When you had expression, you were safe at any speed, anywhere; you could turn pain to understanding like straw into gold.

Knowing this, and Elayne's schedule at the hospital, she went to see Amir. He was standing in the lighted doorway when she drove up. Listening to the katydids, she supposed. He had an eager, child's heart, she could see.

"Hi," she said. "My parents had a fight."

"A fi-ight?" Amir found the English language infinitely amusing. He made a boxing feint and planted his hand on the door frame over her shoulder, smiling.

"I think they're crazy," she said, looking down.

He lifted her chin with a finger. "Cray-zee," he said, rolling his eyes. She didn't like his closeness so much now, but went in with him anyway, not wanting to be timid. The house was all pink and ruffles, and she had to push some pillows off the couch just to sit down. Amir set his beer on the television, where Joan Crawford, without volume, was adjusting her hat.

"It's so sad," Kate said. "They do love each other, you know, but they . . ."

He kissed her, interrupting. He would be hurt if she went on talking about herself and didn't respond. And his country was nearly at war. She put her arms around his neck. He turned the light off with one hand and reached under her sweatshirt with the other.

"Pillows," he said, "too much pillows."

She twisted to pull the heart-shaped one out from underneath. Amir's face in the TV light had lost all its warm color, but she tried to smile.

"What are you thinking?" she asked.

"Thinking?" He was struggling with her belt buckle, and she reached to help. She *believed* in passion.

"Zipper?"

Kate unzipped. In Turkey they wouldn't violate the sanctity of love with words. The couch was too short, so Amir got stranded atop her as he tried to reach into her jeans, then bumped his head on Elayne's doily-covered end table. Wasn't this the way of all life? The sight of him, mute, helpless, full of want, filled Kate's heart to overflowing.

"I love you," she said, and held him so tightly he couldn't move at all.

Over the insects she heard a car approach.

"Amir, a car," she said.

"I too," he said, laughing uncomfortably before the translation formed. "A car!" he said, and leapt to his feet, swearing in Turkish.

They were zipped and sitting by the time Pop knocked. As Amir went to the door, he turned up the TV.

"Your mother sent me," Pop apologized. Hardly a threat, but when he held his hand out to Amir, Amir flinched. Pop looked at his own hand and withdrew it.

"I'm pleased to meet you," he said. "Come on, Kate."

"American television," Amir explained.

"Don't they shake hands over there?" Pop asked when they got home. "I think he thought I was going to hit him." Moths were collecting at the yellow porch light over his head.

"I don't know," Kate said, "we never shook hands."

"I suppose I should speak to you, Kate," Pop said, "but I don't know what to say." She listened to the aimless sound of the brook behind him, waiting for him to go on, but that was all.

"We were only watching TV," she said.

"I'd never doubt you, Kate," Pop said. "You know that."

"Yes," she said. "I do." He pushed the door open for her, turned the light off, and sat back on the swing.

A page turned. Ma was reading, and the light from her half-closed door fell the length of the hall. Kate walked through it to the bathroom. Shame and self-pity flashed over her, in alternate waves, and she rinsed her face over and over until she could see it in the mirror rosy and courageous again. When she stood up, dripping, Ma was behind her.

"You don't come in to say good night, now," she said.

"I thought you were asleep."

"Katie Vanderwald," Ma said, full of scorn. "Katie the Proud lies again. And just like her grandmother, so cool."

"*Please,*" Kate said, so disdainful she startled even herself. Some new authority had blazed up in her in the last few hours, maybe the last few minutes. She turned to shine it straight in Ma's eyes.

Ma smacked her, a blind strike that knocked her against the shower, which gave a resounding, metallic thunder-roll but cushioned the blow.

"My God, Ma!" Kate said. Ma didn't even believe in spanking!

"Don't look at me like that," Ma said. "That didn't hurt you. Get downstairs and do the dishes, you . . . you . . ." Kate started down. "Slut," her mother finished under her breath at the top of the stairs.

There were no dishes, of course. Ma always did them. Children were not household slaves, she said—they should be out soaking up sun and fresh air, dreaming and storing their strength for later on. Laugh, don't do the dishes! Kate sat at the piano in the dark, pretending to organize her music, until Audie came down and folded her in her protective arms.

Ma was two steps behind her. "Don't you make an ogre out of me!" she cried, swooping at them, batlike, slapping the tops of their bent heads, until Pop came in from the porch, rubbing his eyes.

"My God, are you hitting them?" he asked, and she told him not to dare be reasonable with her and sent them to bed, saying not to wake Chucky and for God's sake not to turn this into a scene.

So up they all went, except Pop, who stayed on the porch until time for the early train.

"No, like this," Mrs. Schnippers said. Her hands were bunches of carrots, but she played softly, sharply. "Might as well go back to the beginning, we're not that far in."

Kate went back. In half an hour she had played half a page, with a mistake in every measure, every time. The notes sat before her as useless as an assortment of old screws. Timid, painstaking, she began again.

"Molto vivace, remember?" Mrs. Schnippers prompted, very, very gently. "That's good, that's on the right track."

It wasn't good. Just because she couldn't play the piano didn't mean Kate couldn't hear her own noise. "I'm sorry," she said, "I can't." Pure will kept her from slamming her full arm down on the keys. The damned notes kept her from the music as surely as her body kept her out of the sky! She labored at the piano for grim hours every day, always too slow or too fast, too weak or too loud. She put her head against her music now and willed herself not to cry.

"It's my fault," Mrs. Schnippers said. "I should have let you play it through."

"No, something's wrong."

Mrs. Schnippers' laugh forgave all. "Yes, something is wrong," she said. "You don't know how to play the piano yet. You will, though. Have you been practicing?"

"All the time," Kate said.

Music ought to be like diving: you should make a wide arc over it, let it swallow you, and emerge triumphant, clean. It was so long since Ma had taught her to dive that she didn't remember the lessons, only the skill.

And she had lost Ma absolutely—Ma seemed to despise her now. The month at home had been hot and silent, with only one visit from Pop. Ma and Kate talked about what needed to be done in the house and why Kate had done it wrong. When the toaster went up in flames, Kate was making toast for her

gluttonous self, in midafternoon. When Chucky got stung by a
wasp, it was during Kate's turn to watch him. What was the
matter with her? Next Ma would come home and find he'd
been squashed in the road.

"She's nuts, that's all," Audie reminded her. In the after-
noons they sat on the flat stones in the brook, watching the
water striders skim by. Audie looked so lucky, her head a neat
blond cap bent over her pink toes, the bottle of polish balanced
within reach on the bank. She was having the pearls restrung
as a surprise for Ma. Chucky was the favorite now, having slept
through the wars, and Ma was teaching him to use a rod and
reel. He sat with his line, miming patience, or ran back to the
island and made fish out of leaves.

Kate was alone with her new knowledge: nothing can be made
right. Doubts came thick as fleas; she pinched one, only to be
stung by another, with never a chance to look up. Amir had
gone back to Ankara without even a phone call goodbye. Kate
lay on the grassy bank and watched the clouds make their rapid
transformations overhead. Like all her ideas, dreams, and plans,
they floated free, far above the confusion below.

Then, last night, Ma had apologized.

"Kate," she said, on her way upstairs, "you forgot to feed the
sheep again."

"I did, right before dinner."

"I can hear them bleating," Ma said. "Is that what it's come
to? You don't even care if they starve?"

Kate shut the piano and went up to the shed. One fat ewe
rested her head on the fence rail, then lifted it to babble. Kate
knelt and hugged her between the rails. She and Audie had
bottle-fed the lambs when the mothers balked, and one touch
calmed them now.

"What's the matter, dopey? Are you trying to bay at the
moon?" Probably it had eaten a poisonous plant, as sheep in
their stupid hunger were wont to do.

"Are you sick?" she asked it. "Are you sad?"

"Kate?" Ma had followed her out. Kate's heart, opened to the ewe, clenched again.

"I'm sorry," Ma said stiffly. Why now? But why anything? The world had lost its order; all its peaceful symmetries were gone. It was too dark to see Ma's face, but the sky above her was full of stars.

"I'm sorry too," Kate lied.

"Thank you," Ma said. She turned and went in. Kate watched her pass through the kitchen, the living room, up by the stairwell window, saw the hall light go off and the bedroom light go on. When she took a breath, it felt like her first, and when the ewe in its wretched softness gave another bleat, she cried.

"Maybe you're working *too* hard," Mrs. Schnippers said. "Be *patient* and *listen*. You'll be surprised." Her orange hair bristled as if she had often been surprised.

Desperate for wisdom, Kate could only hear the words. Listen, she wondered as Mrs. Schnippers went on, how listen? The tomato sauce Mrs. Schnippers was canning could be heard a-bubble on the stove.

Summertime and the livin' is easy,
Fish are jumpin', and the cotton is high.
Oh your daddy's rich, and your ma is good lookin',
So hush, little baby, don' yo' cry.

Kate was home from her lesson, before Ma. Her voice sounded low and thrilling when she was alone and sang just as she felt. Fortified, she turned a stern eye on the counterful of vegetables. Green and yellow squash, tomatoes, corn—the produce of a garden gone mad would have to organize itself into a casserole.

The peaches were so ripe now, they glowed like lanterns on the tree.

Audie came in with a pail of beans.

"Minestrone," she said. "You chop."

The knives were never sharp enough. The tomatoes squished out of her grasp and spurted their seeds on her sleeve. Finally Kate ripped them open with her fingers, admiring their rich red.

"Look," Chucky said, through the screen door. He was carrying a real fish, albeit a small one, cupped between his hands.

"Did you take the hook out yourself?" Audie asked.

"I used the butterfly net," he admitted.

"Ah, well, it's a fish, isn't it?" Kate said, opening the door for him. It swam in the mixing bowl until Ma got home.

"Do you mean to say that after you children were nearly raised in that brook, not one of you knows how to clean a fish?" She shook her head and beheaded the fish, gutted and fried it, and gave everyone a bite.

Then she turned to Kate and with some effort asked if she'd had a good day.

"Nothing special," Kate said, stubborn. Now she didn't spend all day phrasing and rephrasing the march of events for Ma, they didn't seem to be events at all.

"How was the lesson?" Ma seemed determined to reconcile. Forgive her, Kate thought, rise above this. But how forgive a mother?

"I can't play the piano," she said finally, as an excuse, "so I'm in a slough of despair."

"Slough of *despond*," Ma said.

"Depths of despond," Kate told her.

"Depths of despair, slough of despond," Ma said. "Trust me, this is one thing I understand. And *don't* be absurd. Of course you can play the piano. With *your* strength of spirit? Hah!" She waved a hand. "Believe me, if you want to, you'll play the piano. Katie Vanderwald," she said, as if announcing a visiting queen, "you have a history of getting what you want, after all." She raised an eyebrow, and the old accusation became praise.

"If you say so," Kate said. "You seem to be objective."

Then she decided to believe her. When the world spins as it does, what is there to do but grab hold? To Audie, smiling at Ma's words now with the familiar shy pride, Kate would always be venerable.

So she would have to do well. After dinner Chuck and Audie raced out to turn cartwheels over the lawn, as they had all three used to do. Then Kate went back to the piano. She played the first page with her whole heart and a thousand errors, then flat and lifeless with every note exact. Then the first three measures, ten times over. Outside, Ma laughed with the children, whose cries had got the sheep bleating and startled a goose out of the brook. Haydn gave order to everything if only you played him right. Kate began again.

Packing Up

Kate wakes up in full darkness, at the first snap of a flame. It can't be a fire—the house is built of the same stone as the crumbling walls that stretch into the hills around it; it leaks, ivy creeps in through the chinks to grow up the window frames, but it is hardly likely to burn. Kate can never sleep in a strange place, for fear of fire. She has kept away so staunchly, studying over vacations, taking distant summer jobs, that home seems unfamiliar, full of perils now. *Sleep*, she says to herself, nearly aloud. She has to be sharp with herself, or she'll be all sloth and fear. Listen. She hears nothing but the slow pulse of tree frogs over the marsh. Dread will not yield, though, and she holds her breath, dares not move lest she miss another sound.

There have been fires: chimney fires, a lightning strike, coals burst free from the hearth. But after the first fright, the frantic phone calls and firemen swarming, all ends in laughter, gin on the porch. Nothing ever really burns.

Even the divorces have been false alarms. Pop, woken from his customary daydream, would be shocked: was something wrong? Ma was always magnificent in rage; she'd take Grace, sweep Chucky from his playpen, buckle them into the Jeep, and escape. A few lost, surreal days at home, Kate and Audie tending to Pop, until the phone rang. Then the tears and apol-

53

ogies, and Pop, restored, full of faith, would see infinite promise in . . . soybeans, or winter wheat. Someday, he said, the market would change their lives. Calling from his office, one eye on the board, he would spin out his plans: a few months of good fortune, and they would sail for the Maldives, buy their own island, live in the trees. Kate and Audie would be set studying Swahili while Ma learned to pound her own flour. Only the market was unwilling. Suddenly they'd be broke again, the dream exploded, the house remortgaged, and Ma, betrayed, off again on the road.

Now the bank is repossessing the house. They—Ma and Pop and the younger children—have known it all spring, though they didn't tell Kate till today. After twenty years safe in the path of disaster, it must have been hard to believe one had come. They continued their perpetual rhythms: feeding the sheep, planting the garden, meeting Pop's train from New York, waiting for the usual reprieve. Now the peas are blooming, the spirea blooms in cascades, and in four days they will have to leave.

Kate has been finishing her last year of college. She's grown too far from them—she vowed long ago to go step by step ahead, not round and round in their little mire of dreams. When the bottom dropped out of beet sugar, she did not quit school; she found, instead, a job, a scholarship, a loan. Every semester had been shaky (the exorbitant school had been chosen in a boom-time mood), but between luck and labor she had got through, and as she waited her turn that morning, in the line of graduates filing from the stage, she half-expected Fate to lift her up in His strong arms and carry her away. Yes, she could see it: a stiff wind would come up under their robes, wafting them up together like a flock of birds, carrying them on various currents into their various lives. She would land far, far from her parents' preserve—in Paris, she thought, defiant in her triumph, and not just Paris but the Paris of Baudelaire.

She had felt as if she *would* fly, down the lawn to the great striped canopy that billowed over the gathered throng. Instead, though it hardly befitted her new status, she ran, one hand holding the mortarboard steady, the other keeping hold of her robe.

But they were broken into factions already. Pop, pale and grave, kept to the edge of the crowd, while Ma, holding Chucky by the hand, had appropriated its center. Among the other, decorous mothers, she burned with electrical intensity, leading Audie and Grace in a wave of proud, indiscreet laughter, staking a rebellious claim. Away from their domain, they seemed like night creatures exposed. Garish, alarming, they blinked and clung to each other, fending off the unfamiliar world.

"Here we are, Katie!" Ma called.

"Pop's over there!" Kate said. She stood midway between them, thinking they'd been separated by accident, but nobody moved. The sun cast wide stripes of light through the tent top, kindling a thousand cups of red punch.

Finally Grace broke from Ma's side. She was fourteen, taller than Kate now and gangly as telescoped Alice, but she had a new delicacy too: she took Kate's arm more in solace than in celebration.

"I'll talk to Pop," she said, "and when you've been with Ma awhile we'll trade."

"What's wrong?" Kate had asked, impatient, wondering why they couldn't let their angers rest just for the day.

Grace was so accustomed to dividing herself equally between her parents, passing their messages back and forth at the dinner table, that she hardly noticed they never spoke to each other, only to her. She was a mass of scruples, part of her adolescent independence. Everything must test for loyalty and good intention, and Kate's vexation failed.

"What do you mean?" Grace asked hotly, and fell under her own censure: this was Kate's day. Kate watched her cautious face relax until the child appeared again, shy and smiling.

"Congratulations!" She threw her arms around Kate's neck and sent the mortarboard flying.

Audie, of course, was the one to explain. Married, like her parents, at nineteen, she had become everyone's confidante and could speak—winding her program around strong, uncertain fingers—of deeds and litigations, Ma's accusations, Pop's rebuttals, the process server, and the price of land.

"So," she said finally, "we have to be packed in four days. It's hard to believe it. It's hard to say it out loud."

"Four days?" said Kate, but checked herself. "Fine." She would refuse even to pity them this time. She was in the hands of Fate. Everyone must blaze ahead today.

Audie took a moment to come around. "I suppose . . ." she said. Then her trusting, rascal's smile, her little sister's will-to-agree. "They *are* impossible."

Grace, baffled by this wicked camaraderie, had set her face. From behind them, a squeal: "Oh, Dad-ee!" as some beaming father dangled a new set of keys.

Grace's room is still neat as a jewel box in the midst of the muddled house, and Kate imagines she is sleeping soundly there. Audie, who is home to help with the packing, is across from Kate in her old bed, an ark of stuffed animals, her hand closed tight on a velvet opossum's tail. If she would wake up, they could whisper as they used to, watching a jar of fireflies on the sill. Ma used to let them stay up as late as they liked: she was afraid of the night with Pop away. In the morning she'd say school wasn't important—they should turn over and go back to their dreams.

Kate dreamed of a larger world than this! She would struggle awake and run up the dirt road out of the valley to catch the school bus: that vessel might teem with threats and humiliations, but it carried her away. In these last years she had come home only for Christmas, and when she thought of the place she saw winter: the house gray as the sky, the brook a sharp black schism through the white land. Summer at home, picking chokecherries for jam—stained fingers, hawkweed soft on her legs as she waded toward the bushes at the edge of a field—still seemed too seductive, a memory they would use to hold her here with them while the weeds grew in the gutter and the willow roots wound up through the pipes. She had planned, after Commencement, to stay for two weeks only, drinking coffee on the lawn with Ma. Then she would lift her arms and let Fate carry her away.

Now she has four days. Driving home after the ceremony, she tried to make new plans: she had three hundred dollars and could double it by selling her car; she could drive to New York, land on a friend's doorstep, go from there. At every fork she considered, but she always turned for home. Highways became streets, the town dwindled, and finally she turned down the narrow road so little traveled that lilacs and elderberries arched over the stone fences alongside, almost touching overhead.

Audie and Grace, ahead of her by only an hour, were packing already, the blond and the dark heads leaning from the upstairs window, long arms throwing blankets out to Pop, who caught each bundle and tossed it into the Jeep. Something had stung them into action, and Kate realized, just from the daze Ma always left behind her, that she must already be gone. The girls seemed unwilling to break their rhythm of labor even to welcome Kate, and she stood before the massive stone porch pillars, uncertain as an immigrant: she was no longer one of them. When they left the window for more, Pop came to embrace her.

"We're so proud," he said, looking through her. He was never one to fix on the present, and Kate was used to checking over her shoulder only to realize he was picturing the curve of a rising market, or a sail on a distant sea. Now he was seeing the past, some hallowed recollection—this farm, the first of his dreams. Kate touched his shoulder, to make herself real.

"Where are we moving?"

Before he could shake himself into the present, Grace was at the window again. "We don't know!" she said. "Catch!" Like parachutes, like wide white wings, the sheets unfurled overhead.

Drifting, half dreaming, Kate pieces the day back together. Sheets and scholar's robes; then a maple leaf floats down on a fishhook; a little cracked pitcher Ma always loved appears, full of terror suddenly, Made in Hell. "Sleep, dopey," she tells herself, in her mother's voice. "Tomorrow you have to pack all day."

Once, Ma had waked them at midnight and taken them out to watch a comet from a blanket on the garden lawn. She and Pop had been fighting all day while Kate and Audie dodged around them, tiptoeing down the back staircase, devising secrets under the porch while Ma, above them, yanked the clothes from the line. Dinner passed in livid silence until one of the sheep nosed open the screen door and tottered toward them, its feet clicking and sliding on the linoleum tiles. Confounded, unable to turn, it gaped at them in dumb sheep-horror and wet the floor.

This had been Ma's last straw: she sprang up in fury, but she was full of love for the sheep.

"Here, baby," she said, sinking her hands deep into its wool, laughing as she coaxed it outside.

"Eat your dinner," she said to Pop. "I'll be mopping up sheep piss." She threw the faucets wide open to fill the bucket, then, overcome, hurled it to the floor, splashing them all with a sudsy wave. She smacked the swinging door open with one flat hand and escaped, sobbing, Pop behind her, while the children sat still as statues, watching the door flap back and forth in their wake.

Waiting for the comet, leaning back against Pop's knee, Ma had laughed easily again, low and confidential, blowing smoke as mosquito repellent into Kate's hair. Another storm was past, forgotten. Grace in her sleepsuit pointed to a blinking jet, but Pop had ruler and compass to show where the star must emerge.

"Three minutes," he said, "two and a half."

The peonies glowed in the garden. Kate didn't remember the comet, only the flowers, when she woke in her bed the next morning. Someone must have carried her in.

She expects grapefruit for breakfast, as if grapefruits grew on the trees outside the kitchen window, weighing them down. Pop, unrolling his nautical charts at the table, had prophesied such things. But there is no grapefruit, nor bread, nor even coffee. Leaks have buckled the oak floorboards in a high ridge the length of the room, and Kate trips, though she means to step over. In the sink are three cups and one tea bag, which she steeps and squeezes to a pale brew, carrying her cup to the lawn. Solitude was always the real luxury here.

Shouts, clattering, laughter, and something comes bumping down the flagstone path, pursued by Audie and Grace and their two shaggy, prancing dogs. It is a wheel come loose from the pony cart, and when the path turns in front of the house, it continues straight along to Kate and thuds down. Audie, breathless, flops beside it while the dogs set upon Kate, licking her, sniffing her, spilling her tea.

"Go away!" She strikes blindly, in a flash of rage, and the blow shames her. Both dogs go yelping, one in pain, one in fear.

"What's the matter with you?" Grace is standing above her, more confused than aggrieved.

"I'm covered with tea."

"We've been working for two hours . . ." Grace's voice thins in plaintive anger: What's wrong with everyone? Why doesn't Kate just pitch in?

"I was asleep," Kate says. Let them pack. This isn't her home anymore. These kitchen plays grow ever more reckless, but soon Ma will be back, the mortgage will miraculously be paid. They'd be luckier if they really could leave.

"Pop needs us," Grace says. "How could Ma go now? She says it's all Pop's fault." She gives a little, stifled cry—this tangle of injustice will not yield. "She took Chucky, and she wanted me to go too and just leave Pop alone."

Audie will go home to her husband, and Kate is long, long gone. Grace is the only one left.

Grace sees their silence as censure. "Pop doesn't have anyone at all. She shouldn't have gone. And she shouldn't have taken *his* car." She gives a hopeless glance at the Jeep, the enormous old getaway car, which does seem a droll excess, rusty at its edges but still a brilliant emerald-green. The contents of the linen closet have filled it completely; the frayed tires compress beneath their load.

"We're renting a U-Haul," says Audie. "Forty dollars a day and five hundred miles free."

"Five hundred miles? Where's he going?" Kate asks. And where is *she* going? They all just assume she has plans.

Audie, from the habit of forbearance, has become the very Dr. Johnson of gesture: her face purses with worry and amusement while her hands fly out to the winds.

"*He doesn't know*," Grace says. "We should all be together now. It's not fair." She covers her face, which is suddenly distorted by tears. It's not long since she swore she'd never leave her mother, even for school. "I don't mean . . ." she goes on. She takes a deep breath, reining herself in, kneeling down between the two dogs, who have settled a safe distance from Kate. "I know Ma's upset. We all are."

Kate tests herself for upset, but it's as if she's only watching. "I am imperturbable," she thinks. Her education will act as a shield. This is just a loss, after all, like other losses. They don't even have to look beyond these fifty acres to find sorrows greater than their own. The first owners, planning to farm, had pulled these stones—enough to build the house and miles of walls— out of a soil so thin it never supported a crop. In the pasture behind the house, boulders larger than men still stand, while the fields are grown back to forest, still marked into squares by stone walls. The old road up the hillside is lost in brush and woodland. At the top there's a log cabin built by a soldier shell-shocked in the First World War. No one knows what became of him. When Kate and Audie climbed in through the ruined window, they found the torn curtains still blowing, a teacup broken in the sink. A birch tree has grown up through the chassis of the soldier's Model T.

Now the forest will cover their traces too. The historians must submit to history. Kate wants to see this day clearly, through scholar's eyes, but last night's snarled dreams hang over her like a caul.

"Yes, honey," Grace says, kneeling between the dogs, stroking one, then the other. "Yes, everything's all right, everything will be just fine."

Silent, side by side in the living room, they load books into boxes and carry them out to the porch.

"We have to go faster," Audie says. Pop, adrift in the muddle, is carrying a kerosene lamp back and forth, looking for the perfect box, rejecting them all. Kate, at the bookshelf, reads random passages, testing her new wits. These books have always seemed just part of the wall, their titles—*Far from the Madding Crowd*, *The Gathering Storm*—promising revelations; it is surprising now to find they yield up secrets plain as jinxed love and war.

"Like this." To demonstrate, Audie pulls out half a shelf at once, dumps it into a box, and goes back for more. Nothing is in order. The house smells of mildew and neglect, as if it had long since been given up for lost. The attic, the cellar, the barn are jammed with things like automatic chicken-feed dispensers, old ticker-tape machines. By midafternoon they have packed one room. A spider tends its thick web in the corner above them, and Kate brushes the back of her neck, feels through her hair.

"These old tools were here when we bought the house," says Pop from the hall closet. "Look, Grace, this works with a spring action, do you see?" He brings out an enigmatic contraption and takes it apart. Grace tries to look interested, though she's reaching deep to the back of a shelf to pull out a nest of rags.

"An apple corer. We found it in the henhouse with the old sharpening wheels," he says. "You weren't even around then, Baby Sister, and Audie was just about to be born."

Audie telegraphs a warning to Kate. If he sinks into nostalgia now, there'll be no retrieving him. Before they can change the subject, though, he has opened the cupboard of Christmas ornaments. He turns from it as if from a rebuke and sits down.

"You know," he says, "there was enough land here that you could each have had a little parcel. We could have built two houses up by the waterfall and one over on the hill. It wouldn't have to be elegant, we'd be together. I'd visit my grandchildren . . ."

Audie and Grace leave their work to comfort him, repeating the gentle phrases "Don't worry . . . we love you," like a rosary, one on each side of his chair. Kate opens the book in her hand and vows to live by whatever sentence she finds, but it's an investment adviser. She has just fitted a tiny leather volume of Shakespeare into an empty space, and she plucks it up again, closing her eyes to choose a page.

"Forbear, and eat no more!" Orlando cries.

"Okay," says Pop, breaking, renewed, from the daughterly

embrace, "okay." He is blithe by nature, trained to see the windfall just ahead; sorrow unnerves him.

"Let's go jump in the brook," he says. "Come on, it's too hot for this." He yanks Grace's braid and chases her, squealing, down through the field. Kate and Audie watch from the windows as he lifts her, as if to heave her in, then tenderly sets her down on her feet in water only a few inches deep.

"How are we going to get this done?" Audie says, hand, as ever, on hip. "Steve needs me at home."

She loves him as Kate imagines their parents loved, at nineteen: inextricably. Audie loves the shopping malls now and holds forth on triple-A baseball with a small, bustling pride. She cooks and cleans and clips coupons while his jeans billow from their fire-escape clothesline like flags. Kate understands it, fearfully well. It's an undertow—"I love you" is the last choking cry. Her lover at school appears in her dreams as a raven, a shape torn out of darkness, swooping down to fix her in his golden eye. Once, she had come upon him in the library, his whole body tensed over a sentence. She had wanted to rip Nietzsche out of his hands: "Study me!"

"You should go home," she tells Audie, who is rummaging in the closet again and emerges with a khaki uniform and a pair of scuffed saddle shoes. She examines these items suspiciously, as if her parents might still be inside.

"If we leave it to them, it'll never get done," she says to Kate, with a smile of regretful wisdom. It's just the two of them again, as it always used to be: ministers under a mad monarchy, meek and still and secretly in charge.

Audie finds a can of shrimp, and they add it to macaroni salad for supper. She steps instinctively over the buckled floor, cooking and packing at once, while Kate considers how to keep things from breaking, wrapping a few glasses in a quarter of an hour. At the porch table they eat in silence. Grace has braided her wet hair, and it makes a mark on her sundress that grows wider as they sit.

Audie's face is smudged, and a long scratch runs up her left arm. She eats in a moment and stands up to clear away.

"Whoa, wait a minute," Pop says. "Take it easy there, Audiekins, I just got started."

"I thought . . ."

"Don't think," he says, smiling, his eternal spring of jollity welling again. "Cool it. Enjoy the breeze." When she sits, he claps a hand to her head until she relaxes.

"We've got a perfect summer evening here," he says, and Kate follows his gaze over the brook to the hillside, where he's been clearing the road up to the falls. It's taken twenty years to cut just through the blackberries and birches to the old field, where the road ends in a tangle of thistle and brambly rose. Kate has always brought anyone who mattered here, walking them up the road and through the layers of forest to see the water fall free over the ledge. Once a buck came crashing through a thicket not three feet in front of her: snorting, tossing its antlers, nothing like the does who stole down in the evenings to drink, it galloped once around the clearing before her and plunged back into the brush. Kate catches her breath again, fixing the memory. She will want to describe this place someday, trying to explain herself.

Audie is poised at the edge of her chair, awaiting Pop's permission to stand, but Grace gives her a wary glance: he told them to relax.

"Do you want a drink?" she asks him, running inside and returning in a moment to the porch window, passing him a gin and tonic in a jelly glass, the lime pierced, as he has taught her, on the rim.

"I'm sorry," she says. "The crystal is all packed."

Absorbed in the hillside, he gives a weak, fond smile, but the first sip revives him.

"You girls want to go to a movie tonight?"

"You're joking." The minute Audie says it, she covers her mouth at contradicting him. But they never go to the movies. The theater is an hour away.

"Certainly not. Grace, run get the paper and we'll see what's on."

"We'll probably all feel better if we make some progress tonight," Audie says carefully.

"We'll *definitely* all feel better if we take a little break," says Pop. Grace returns to the window without the paper.

"I wrapped the crystal in it," Kate tells him.

"Then we shall blaze off into the great unknown, eh, Baby Sister?" Pop starts singing: "Pack up your troubles in your old kit bag . . ."

"We *can't*," says Audie.

Pop's smile is full of love, and utterly obtuse.

"Don't say 'can't,' honey," he says. "Anything might happen. Where would you like to live next? The Spice Islands?" He leans back and laces his fingers behind his head, preparing to ruminate. "I know things have been shaky, but I think . . . most people disagree, but *I* think there's going to be a turnaround, and if the past few days are any indication . . ."

The sibylline market.

"Rice terraces!" he says. "Shimmering in the equatorial sun . . ." He holds a hand out toward this consoling vision, watching Audie to see if she will follow him there. "Sandalwood forests . . . what do you suppose that movie will be, Baby Sister, *South Pacific?*"

"Well," says the patient Audie, "it does sound wonderful, but I guess I'll just stay here and do a few little things." Pop, on his way in for his sweater, is still humming and doesn't hear.

"We *have* to go with him," Grace says. "He's just cheering up." She climbs delicately over the windowsill and goes down the stone steps to sit, prim, in the passenger seat of the Jeep, facing the brook, away from them.

Suddenly they hear a car, coming too fast, kicking up stones on the dirt road. This sound is so rare, it is ominous. When they were children, Kate and Audie would dive together to the ground behind the stone wall, lest they be seen. Instinct still tells Kate to duck. Ma pulls the Buick up into the driveway beside the Jeep.

"Where's your father?"

He comes to the door. Kate and Audie are trapped on the porch between them. Just from the tilt of Grace's head, Kate guesses that she has determined to be valiant again.

"Hi, Ma," she says from the Jeep window, in a voice so wary of offending it is absolutely flat. "You came back."

Ma seems neither to hear nor see her, coming up the steps still in her baggy gardening clothes. She's in the eye of a black rage, single-minded, silent, and cold.

"I need my things," she says, but Pop keeps his arm across the door.

"Lila," he says. It's an appeal, kind and sorrowful.

"*What?*" She sounds utterly disgusted, but she's listening. Kate hardly dares to blink. He could say anything now.

"Be reasonable, Lila," he says.

"Oh, yes, I forgot." Ma swells with bitter scorn. "I'm not *reasonable*. I will *not* pull myself together. You take everything . . ." She gestures toward the garden, where she used to kneel in the dirt for whole summer mornings, dreamily weeding. The full, loose peony blossoms weigh heavy on their stems.

". . . everyone," she says, widening the sweep of her arm to include Audie and Katie and Grace. "Just let me go. Let me pass, Gil."

He stands aside, follows her in. The storm door slams behind him.

"Remember when she threw the iron out the window at him?"

Audie asks. Realizing they're alone again, she and Kate start to laugh. They can hear the argument continuing inside, in cadences so familiar it is almost comforting.

"Remember when he gave her a ride to the lawyer?" Audie says. They had once driven off to seek a divorce together, but Ma kicked Pop so furiously he went off the road into a telephone pole. By the time his arm was set, a bottomless tenderness had opened between them—it lasted for most of a year.

"That was the summer we got the sheep," says Audie. For her this is no dream of the country; it's home. Kate remembers her as a child in her fawn-colored jacket, pockets ripped loose, swinging by her knees from a low branch so her long hair brushed the ground.

Inside, Pop is recalling the old days too, his weekends at home with them, the children racing over the evening lawn. They can hear him so clearly he must be calling his stories up the stairs to Ma.

She returns crying, her arms full of clothes. Pop is behind her, picking up dropped socks. He touches her shoulder.

"Don't!" She flinches, dropping more things, stoops to collect them, drops even more, but when Kate goes to help her, she recoils and sweeps everything together with one majestic arm.

"You'd better get to work, girls," she says, mocking them, as she carries her bundle down the steps to the car. By helping him, by sitting here on the porch with him, they have betrayed her. It is becoming difficult to trace the great web of betrayal, except to see that loyal Grace, who is still waiting for Pop in the Jeep, is caught at its center now.

"And don't tell me, Grace," Ma says, "that we should all work together. This was your father's idea, and it's his job."

"Which he can't do without *his* car," Grace blurts.

Kate expects to hear her scolded for back talk, but Ma is so unhappy she cannot rise to authority.

"*I* paid for this car," she says. "You're not coming, I gather."

Grace looks quickly up to the porch at Pop, who doesn't move. "You're not *staying*," she replies. It's an entreaty, but Ma turns away.

"I won't forget this, Grace," she says, monumentally cold. She throws her things into the back of the Buick, gets in, and slams it into reverse.

The sound, as the two cars smack together, is not particularly loud among the day's other noises, and Kate can see Ma means to ignore it, but the Jeep rocks on its high wheels and lurches forward onto the lawn. From here it is a long, straight slope to the brook. The Jeep rolls slowly, stately, as in a dream, with Grace still inside.

"Step on the brake!" Kate yells, but of course Grace has never even tried to drive a car. She sits perfectly still, looking ahead of her toward the brook and the woods beyond. The bank is high, the Jeep unsteady . . ."

"Gracie, jump out!" Kate calls. Nothing happens, and no one else seems alarmed. They watch transfixed as the silent wheels press down the lawn, gathering speed, clipping off fat white peony blossoms as they go. Pop is looking at Ma as if this were another of their everyday spectacles, as if what happens will occur on her face. They think they are charmed, Kate thinks, safe in their Arcadian valley, apart from the world and time.

Perhaps they are right. The Jeep passes between the twin maples neatly as if someone were steering, and though it rocks as it goes over the bank, it does not tip. It turns with the current, seeming to begin a long journey, and floats a few feet before it becomes mired. Grace opens the door, takes off her shoes, and, holding up the hem of her dress, steps into the water, stopping to rinse the mud off her feet before she comes up the lawn.

"That's my Gracie, always cool," Ma says, still mocking, but there is something—in her face, in her tone—a hint of amusement, of pride. She shakes her head; she almost smiles.

Pop leans back against one of the porch pillars, smiling for real.

"You see," Kate whispers to Audie, "we'll never be rid of each other." Life will go on with the same rages and sorrows, plans and disappointments, the same freedom among the leaves. And this is as it should be. Kate feels, finally, as if she has never been away, as if college were just another of those grand dreams from which you awake yourself still at home.

As soon as she sees Grace safe, though, Ma gets back into the Buick. Slowly now, with not a flourish, not a word, she backs around and drives away. For a moment Kate doesn't understand; then she sees—from Pop's and Audie's faces—that this is it at last, the real, quiet thing. When they can no longer hear the car, Pop drinks down his gin and goes inside.

"It's just that it isn't fair," Grace says, coming up the porch steps, shoes in hand.

"We know, honey," says Audie fondly. Even she seems suddenly uncertain, unprepared.

"This is rueful," Kate thinks. "Now I am full of rue." It is the hour of her old lonely ritual: she would escape them, after dinner, to walk around the upper field, looking down over the yellow-lit house in the valley with its spruce bulwark against an incandescent sky. She could feel infinitely tender toward the house and its dwellers, from her distant rise. For all her pursuit of the world beyond, her studies, this land, these people are all she really knows.

"Where are you going next week?" Audie asks. "Do you want to stay with us for a while?"

No one else has remembered. Grace pokes her toe into a knothole in the floor. "Maybe you ought to go with Ma."

"We've got lots of room," Audie says. "We're looking for a couch in the classifieds."

"Merci beaucoup," Kate says, because in English she would probably cry.

"That's right, you know French now," says Audie, with such wondering admiration that Kate knows she ought to say—in a French so vividly expressive anyone could understand—something wise and gentle, something so true that this moment will ignite before it, burn to ash, and blow away.

"Yes," she says, "now I know French." She starts to gather up the dishes, but once Audie has taken Grace in, she leaves them and goes down the steps to the lawn: to try, finally, to print the place sharp in her mind. Peony petals are strewn in the ruined garden. The Jeep faces resolutely downstream while the willows around it fill with the last light. The light gilds everything—deep woods and bramble and swamp—and this will be her memory, she knows. She won't remember the true thing, the din of irreconcilable emotion; she'll remember how she wished it could be. The insects are setting up their low rhythms, calling and answering. The boulders throw ancient, familiar shadows over the field. The house might be one of them: it stands like a stone lion against the hill. If Kate could be sure no one saw her, she'd kneel.

Shoe

I've never seen a picture of my grandfather, but in my idea of him he's not old. I've never seen a photograph, even a poster of a movie star, that can compete with my image of him: very dark in every way, moving powerfully but fluidly, without great thought or care. I believe he's too powerful to be elegant, but that he appears elegant when he wears a suit, that his elegance is assumed with the suit. He's tailored, mustached, composed, a perfect line drawing of a man.

He once designed a famous building, the New York office of the Bank of the Lesser Antilles. He fought in World War II, was in Paris when the city fell. He grew up in Maine, one of a fatherless family of fourteen, living on potato soup. Somewhere in upstate New York a town is named for him: L'Eglisier. These are facts, but they may not pertain to my grandfather. I've heard them or overheard them, but when I repeat them, I suspect myself of lying: if I'm talking to an architect, I make my grandfather a criminal lawyer or a chef. I know that he lives in Sioux City, Iowa, or in Arizona now that he's retired.

I tell people that I'm a dancer, and I usually feel this is the truth. I'm not a ballerina or a chorus girl but a dancer without the jewels and veils. I study with a well-known master who keeps a studio on the lower East Side of New York. We lean

71

over, curve our backs, swing our arms loose from our shoulders, jutting one hip upward. We topple and thud to the floor. Taught to consider ourselves substantial, we rarely leap. We move "sinuously—like globs of syrup."

I'm not good at what I do. My muscles are naturally tense. I picture Isadora Duncan wistfully as I flop along with the corps.

We have, as an exercise, to find an attitude for one of our grandparents, to "fit our muscles along his or her bones." I choose my grandfather. He walks along Gramercy Park, with his pipe. He is wearing a suit. He stops, standing at the wrought-iron gate, holding the pipe just away from his mouth. His other arm is loose at his side. It is evening, and around him everyone is hurrying. They might as well blur. He stands distinct and relaxed, looking away from the street, into the park. Light slants around him, through the tops of the trees.

When I was a child, perhaps six, I found a shoe in my grandmother's closet. She was a schoolteacher, a woman with many small bottles of perfume and a great number of shoes, all leather, all subdued. Among these was a single shoe, a delightful shoe compared with the others: a high, wedged heel covered in white canvas, stitched all over with glass beads, red and gold and blue. It had no mate that I could find, and it seemed to be a work of art, placed, mistakenly because of its shape, among the shoes.

My mother took it from me before Grandma could see it. Ma's anger has always been cold and terrible. She loses her peripheral vision and sees only the offending act. It is as if she would tear you apart. I stood absolutely silent in front of her, hoping she would overlook me, and she did. She took the shoe straight back to the bedroom, and then she went into the bathroom and took a shower. I climbed up on the back of the couch and pressed my face against my grandmother's window, watching the customers at the deli across the street. When I heard the water stop, I slid down and sat delicately, my feet flat on the floor, a magazine open on my lap.

I am improving the attitude of my grandfather. I think of him in Paris, in uniform. He stands very erect, but easy. My shoulders are loose, one hand rests against the wall in place of the Gramercy Park gate, the other is cupped around the space for a pipe. My eyes are absolutely clear, but I don't see the deep-colored leaves that drift in front of me in the park. He is picturing some scene from the past or the future, not a hazy fantasy but the kind of sharp-edged vision that precedes action. He is entirely absorbed.

One man in the class is lucky. His grandfather was a hunchback. He stoops, and each day the hump is more pronounced. His muscles really work. I am amazed at how close he can come to deformity and how easily he stands up, stretches out, and returns to his own shape.

Some weeks before my mother turned thirty-five, she got a birthday card from my grandfather. It was a "Happy Belated Birthday" card for a child, with a pastel circus tent embossed on it, signed "Love, Dad," with his name in parentheses below.

"My father had a wonderful sense of humor," my mother said. Then she looked at the postmark. "Chicago. I wonder if he lives there." She read the little printed poem on the card out loud, but it didn't seem to mean anything special. She put her arms out to me and held me, and cried.

It was that year, I think, that I found the shoe again. At first I thought it was the mate to the one at Grandma's. I had forgotten the shoe, probably forgotten it the same day I first saw it, but now, discovering it in the back of an old bureau we had stored in the cellar, I remembered my mother's face, distorted with anger, returned to composure only after she came out of the shower, her hair wrapped in a towel that gave her the height of a statue. I did not mention it this time. I reached into the drawer for the shoe and carried it up to my room, where I stuffed it inside one of my own boots. Knowing Ma's response to it, I waited until I was alone with my grandmother.

"Where did you get that?" she said, when she saw the shoe in my hand. I had never heard her speak so sharply.

"It's just like the one at your house," I said.

"There's only one shoe like that," she said. "Give it to me." She took it out of the room, and when she returned, she was kind and befuddled again, asking if I wanted to help her make candied apples.

That night, I sat on the top stair and listened to her arguing with Ma. Grandma sounded tired, frustrated. Over and over again she said, "I don't know." Ma's voice was bitter sarcastic, very low. I could hardly hear it, and what I heard I couldn't understand.

I searched the shoe stores for a pair like the jeweled wedgie I had found, but there were no wedged heels at all that year. When I finally described the shoe to a saleswoman, she went behind the counter and said to the cashier, "Marty, this girl wants a pair of hooker shoes."

I'm at work on the hips, in particular. My grandfather is not a man who would place great emphasis on his hips, I don't think. His shoulders are very sharp, his spine is straight, but his hips are casually at rest. His feet are slightly apart, and his body rises comfortably out of this powerful stance, mannered and elegant with a hard, sure gaze.

My classmates regard me with derisive awe.

"What was this guy, a male model?"

"One of the first," I say. "That's how he put himself through architecture school. It was the Depression, you know."

"Well," says this woman, whose grandmother must have been

a potato farmer, from the attitude she strikes, "maybe you should think of him later in life, give him some more character."

She means to be helpful, I know. "He died in World War II," I say. I don't think of this as a real lie.

"Well, you can't just do a pose. Look how stylized this is." I look into the mirror as she runs her finger along the curve of my outstretched arm. Maybe style was his natural way. "You've really got to get in there and give us his heart," she tells me.

I strive. I know he stands at the fence. I know he's attractive, intriguing to the men and women who pass him, carrying baskets of bread, sausages, and cabbage. The air is stingingly cool, the sweetness of the decaying leaves is masked by an odor of coffee and diesel exhaust. Two children squeeze through a break in the fence, and my grandfather looks above them, outward, making a plan, I think. He's still too stiff, too separate. I sag a little and lose him altogether. I want to be stoop-shouldered and cross-armed, to hang my head. It is his ideas, his emotions, that give him his substance. I don't know how to work backward.

When I was seventeen, my boyfriend went away for the summer and came back engaged to be married. For weeks I was despondent. My mother was despondent for me. We stayed up all night watching late movies, and I shuffled to school exhausted, got high in the parking lot at noon, giggled through French class, and fell asleep in study hall.

One night, in the middle of *Zombies from Beneath the Swamp*, we were picturing the married life of my boyfriend and his fiancée: gray dish towels figured prominently in the discussion. I would get even with them just by letting them live their drab little wedded life. "And," Ma said, laughing, "as a last resort, you can always send her your shoe."

"What?" I said.

We were terribly punchy; she had a pillow over her face and was laughing uncontrollably. She dropped the pillow slightly so she could see me. "Of course, I don't think *those* shoes would do it." She pointed to my desert boots drying beside the fireplace. "It should be something a little risqué, preferably something that reveals some toe." She put the pillow back over her face and laughed.

The zombies had gained entrance to the manor house, and the pretty blond girl sat up in bed suddenly, the silk strap of her nightgown slipping over her shoulder as she screamed.

"That's what your grandfather's mistress did," she said, "and it worked like a charm. Just the shoe, no message, but my mother didn't have much trouble figuring it out. It's not every day that people send single shoes in the overseas mail."

The girl in the silk nightgown was, by now, a zombie. She still looked pretty, but when she tilted her head and turned toward the camera, we could see it: her eyes were dead.

"Of course," my mother said, "she had the shoes for it. Your grandmother had boots. Out went philandering Philip."

"Where did he go from there?"

"Well," she said, "he lived on Gramercy Park for a little while, and he didn't go back to France. That's all I know."

"Don't you wonder where he is?"

"Why? Do you think he wonders about me?" She was quiet for a few minutes. Then she said, "I'm sorry I brought it up."

The next night I stayed up alone.

When my parents were divorced and we moved out of the house, I found the shoe again. It was very well hidden this time, in a barrel of old stuffed toys that had long since been turned into mouse nests. I was alone when I found it, and I packed it with my few clothes and books and took it to New York with me.

———

I can't find an attitude for my grandfather. I know it's supposed to be an attitude, not a pose, I know I should look for his heart. We're not supposed to do research, but I have to resort to it. I find the New York office of the Bank of the Lesser Antilles: it takes up three rooms in a hideous blue-and-white box of a building downtown.

Finally, I take the shoe with me to Little Italy, where I ask people until I find the address of a shoemaker. He lives in an apartment with beaded curtains, beaded radiator covers, and a vat of soup in which whole chickens roll in boiling stock. Yes, he can make another shoe like this. It will cost one hundred dollars. Beadwork is expensive. I talk him down to fifty-five, which still means I have to cancel my dentist appointment. As I leave, he says, "Fifty-five for you only," and pinches my ass quickly twice, once on each cheek. I don't object when he does this; but the next week, when I return to pick up the shoes, I stand in the doorway to hand him the cash, and back all the way to the stairs.

Now that I have the shoes, I have everything. They very nearly match. The beadwork of the older shoe has a harsh glow; I imagine there's gold in the dye. The new pigments are too basic, too exact. I want to run home, but I walk, taking the stairs two at a time all the way up the six flights to my apartment.

I've never asked again about my grandfather, or the shoe. My mother got one more card from him, at Christmas, years after her divorce. Its printed message read:

To wish you loads of Christmas cheer,
And love that grows each passing year.

She threw it out in a pile of sale announcements and grocery circulars, and I didn't bother to retrieve it. It was postmarked

Sioux City, Iowa. Maybe he's a salesman. Or maybe he's been a hog farmer all these years.

In the center of my room I stretched my arm out. I'm my grandfather, at the Gramercy Park gate, in 1945. It's autumn, and the sky is steel-gray, just before dusk. Children play in the park, their coats folded on schoolbooks on the benches. I look out over their heads, over the fallen leaves in the park. I want to feel my muscles drawn into place around some emotion. My grandfather looks out past the gate into the network of color and movement that makes up the city, but he sees the horizon of Sioux City, Iowa: uniform and yellow gray.

I myself see, at this moment, a pair of extravagantly, surpassingly gaudy shoes. I give up on my grandfather and put them on.

They are the highest heels I've ever worn, and the minute I stand in them, my body conforms to their dictates: my ankles tilt forward, and every other bone leans back to balance them. I stretch my arm out, bring the other to my mouth with the imaginary pipe, and I am indeed a ridiculous figure. I walk confidently in these shoes, taller and more fluid, and I cannot possibly move like my grandfather now. I stand straighter than I ever have, my breasts thrust forward against the cloth of my shirt, head back, almost thrown back. If I were to laugh right now, it would be a strong but not derisive laugh that I think my grandfather would attend: the laugh of someone who understands what he looks for and what he sees.

Nonchalant

Kate closed Buddy's up early because of the snow. It took all her strength to pull the door shut against the wind, and she felt herself very slight, almost weightless, her hair blowing to mix with the storm. She wore the red scarf she had knitted for Michael, which he hadn't taken to New York with him. He had said then that he'd be back before the cold, but he no longer spoke of returning. Evidently, fiddle players were much needed in New York; Kate hadn't thought he would get enough work to keep him a month, but he'd left in September and it was nearly Christmas now.

Kate's own work kept her in Chiverton. Buddy said she was the best cook he'd ever had, and at Buddy's she could do things according to her mood, serve coq au vin one night and meatball subs the next, boil an egg if someone was allergic, bake a cake if someone was sad. Only Michael had escaped her ministrations, though his name was still on her mailbox and she was still watering his plants.

So let him stay in New York. Carson had a formula for it: If someone has lived away from you as long as they've lived with you (and if the distance is one hundred miles or more), you can't consider yourself in love. Kate tried to be nonchalant—Michael had been mostly a pain in the ass anyway, schlepping home from some woman's apartment with a camellia for Kate, his confessions so detailed he seemed not so much penitent as nostalgic. He had invited her to come to New York with him, but so halfheartedly it would have seemed importunate to accept.

Even in the light of the evening snow, Chiverton was a dingy town, whose tinseled storefronts still displayed the galoshes and baby dolls no one wanted last year. Three blocks east and Kate would be home; three more and the town subsided into fields until the valley sloped up into the hills again. The wreath on the door of The Shamrock, where Michael once played three nights a week, obscured most of the neon Schlitz sign, and Kate peered through the letters, thinking she might find Carson or someone else who'd want to walk with her, but there were only a few kids playing Pac-Man. They spent all their aimless force on the machines, unconcerned with the snow, which sifted through the pools of streetlight onto the little spruces along the sidewalk. Watching them, Kate knew she was absolutely lucky to be here, alone, in a red scarf. Carson would say she was feeling negative ions rather than joy, but the snow tumbled freely out of the pure blue above; science had nothing to do with it.

Carson was going bald. When he was eating lunch at Buddy's and Kate stood at the counter, he knew she could see the spiral of missing hair at his crown, and he sorted through the rest of his hair, trying to push some wisps over the empty spots.

"I'm still kind of a handsome guy, don't you think, Katie?" he asked. She was pulling apart a lettuce for salad. "That Annie in the florist is kind of a snack cake, don't you think? And I think she sorta likes your friend Carson here."

Carson wore more than one plaid at a time, and he was developing a beer belly despite heroic effort, but he was handsome, and when Kate looked down at his pleading face, she smiled. She knew everyone thought they were lovers. Sometimes she thought so herself.

"You are unquestionably the handsomest regular customer at Buddy's," she told him, "and Annie's a real Twinkie."

"Wait," he said, as she went back into the kitchen. "Katie, wait. What do you mean, regular? What kind of stranger's been coming in here behind my back?" While Kate was trying on several enigmatic looks, in came Terri Brinn, who worked with Carson at the hospital.

"Terri, is there anyone you know—and be honest, I mean really, you can be totally honest—but do you know anyone who can really be said to equal the Carson charm?"

Terri regarded her engagement ring with some distress, but finally said, "Hi, Carson. Hi, Katie," and went to sit at the end of the counter, on the other side of the mailman. Terri lived in the apartment below Kate's, but she had moved in after Michael left, so she, like everyone else, had the wrong impression about Carson. She smiled apologetically as Kate told her the specials. Kate smiled sweetly back at her. Terri would just murder her Don if he seemed to care about another woman's opinion of him.

"Who is it?" Carson was saying. "You can tell me, Katie. I know you, Katie, and it's probably some big dumb goof who hasn't got nearly the Carson savoir faire." Almost everyone was looking by now, and Kate began to feel she actually had betrayed him.

"It's nobody, Carson. It was a slip. You are by far the most gorgeous hunk of man who's ever slurped his soup at this counter, who's ever deigned to pick his teeth with one of Buddy's toothpicks here."

"I don't know, Katie, you don't say that with any conviction."

"Oh, *Carson.*" Kate leaned over the counter and spoke quietly to him, exasperated and laughing. "You know I think you're wonderful."

"Listen, this other guy didn't go in the flower shop, did he?"

It occurred to Kate that Annie would have been the one who suggested camellias healed all wounds, and she stood up to go back to the kitchen.

"Carson, I'm not thinking of anyone in particular."

"Oh, I get it," he said. "Michael, right?"

"Carson, shush. Please?"

"I get it," he said. The mailman paid for his piece of quiche, taking a toothpick and looking as if he felt a little sad about not being the handsomest man at Buddy's. Kate was careful to touch his hand as she took his money, to smile right into his eyes.

"You can't be in love with a dead horse, Katie," Carson said. "Step over it and go on." A familiar argument, but too sensible to work.

"So what's the pathology report?" she asked.

"What? Oh, on the horse? I haven't read it yet." She always gave him Michael's letters to read. He was, after all, a researcher, and the tortured sentences in which Kate tried to find love he studied with the same reasoning calm he used on white cells devouring each other in a drop of blood.

The snow was an inch thick on the telephone wires, and Terri Brinn, soon to be Terri Brinn Reilly, Mrs. Don, stood on the landing, waiting to ask Kate in for hot chocolate and wedding dress analysis. Kate had never seen her without makeup before, and this new vulnerability (her skin was pocked, but her eyes without the heavy liner were full of shy friendship) became her. Don Reilly's picture dominated her coffee table, as his laugh often dominated the building when he was visiting her. He was a truck driver for a dairy company, and he wore a blue uniform with DON stitched on the breast pocket in red.

"My fiancé says I look best in empire waists," Terry said. *Empire* was a word Kate had never dared to speak, having been told that when used sartorially it was pronounced *ahmpeer*. To hear Terri say "empire" was a relief that nearly made her giggle. Wedding dresses seemed worthy of hours of discussion now, and Kate agreed that Terri would look best in empires, in cap sleeves, in panne velvet and inset lace.

Wedding breakfasts were harder—no pictures—but here Kate had experience. Chicken croquettes looked so stodgy, but lobster bisque was a wonderful color, for February.

"That's soup, isn't it?" Terri said. "Don likes something substantial. Wouldn't Carson want more than soup?"

"Carson eats what I tell him to eat," Kate said. "But you're right. It should be beer and those sausages—bangers, right? Lobster bisque is too prim. A wedding ought to be vital."

"Doesn't the royal family serve chicken croquettes?" Terri asked her.

Michael had been in a state of suavity when Kate was last in New York. His apartment was directly over a fish storehouse, but he served brandy in cut glass, had flowers—daisies, not camellias—on the table in a beer mug. The quartz heater glowed like a fireplace, and he even had presents for her, things he had been saving for weeks. She couldn't imagine him seeing a bunch of silk ribbons in a store window, thinking of her, turning back to buy them.

Hardly any subject was comfortable. "What's V.S.O.P.?" she asked.

"Very Superior Old Panacea," he said. She allowed a wan smile.

She stretched her legs toward the heater. "What does it mean: 'Heats the surface without heating the air'?" she asked.

"Physics," he said, annoyed. "It's just an advertising gimmick."

The moon, which had been hanging over the Chock Full o' Nuts sign across the river, dropped into New Jersey. On Michael's dresser was a collection of barrettes, expensive ones in the shapes of leaves, threaded with gold. Kate said nothing. She felt suave too. She didn't feel natural with him until they were making love.

The next days were better. They went walking, around the construction area that was destroying the view from his apartment, down to the fish market, and through all the accessible areas around the harbor. Boarded-up warehouses that had seemed abandoned turned out to be in use, full and quiet. In the grocery store Michael told the manager about her job at Buddy's, saying that she made Chiverton seem cosmopolitan. The man had never heard of Chiverton.

The last night, the moon never rose, but a cruise ship came by so fully lit it looked like a new borough. She stood at the window, watching it, feeling ready to put her hand through the glass, ready to do anything that would break the reserve between them. When he came to stand behind her, anger, fear, and desire kept her still—she wanted both to move toward him and away.

Asleep, he pulled her toward him, trapped one of her legs between his, held her head against his chest. The wind slammed a door somewhere over and over, and Michael spoke in his sleep every time Kate moved or even breathed deeply, saying, "What? What?" as if she were keeping something from him. Awake, he never answered her questions. She thought of oil spreading out over water, wishing something in her could cover him that completely and flexibly. "What?" he said, and she stayed still, staring at the ceiling, wanting to sit up and give him a long, full answer, to talk and talk, telling him what. But she was afraid to wake him, and she wasn't sure she knew.

Falling asleep, Kate had the sense that the snow weighed everything in Chiverton down, solid and safe. The sheets were cool against her skin, and she stretched across the whole bed, glad of the solitude, the perfect, snowy quiet. Don arrived downstairs—even his obnoxious laugh was comforting. He called to Terri from the bathroom, pissing torrents. Beer and bangers for this wedding, Kate thought as she fell asleep. She woke again when he was leaving, just before dawn, but before she knew for sure she was awake, she was lost. Don slammed the front door, and her window burst with shooting, blaring light. A ball of fire was outside, moving in.

Terror is the sudden absence of explanation. This had not the properties of a fire or an explosion or even a vision; it assaulted her senses and ignored her mind. Kate was out of the room and down the stairs in seconds, finding Terri and Don in the hall.

"It's a fire," she said. "I don't have anything on."

"God, she doesn't," Don said. Out of hysteria, a reassuring embarrassment emerged.

"It's the electrical cables," Terri said. "I called the fire department." She took off her robe and wrapped Kate in it, so that she was the one undressed, wearing only black panties with pink elephants on them, and matching bra. She pulled Kate upstairs, rewrapped her in one of her bedsheets, and took the robe back. Flashes of electricity spilled through the doorway, lighting their faces weirdly, and static ripped at the air so they had to shout to be heard.

"It's the weight of the snow," Don said. "Those wires were all frayed. This is an old building." He was holding Terri, who shuddered with each new flash. Kate stood against the doorframe, holding the sheet tighter. How could she have gone to bed naked, unguarded, last night?

Carson came in at lunchtime and seemed not to notice any-thing, although Kate was wearing Michael's black corduroys and sweater and had left her hair hanging in tufts over her eyes.

"I've done it," he said. "I've discovered a cure for baldness, and I'm going to win the Nobel Prize." He sat at the counter and twirled around on the stool.

"What about cancer?" Kate wanted to smile, but the fire had made her angry and competent. Already she had fed huge breakfasts to the snowplow operators. She seemed to be gliding; each egg broke cleanly, and masses of them stared up at her from the grill.

"First things first," Carson said, handing her the twist tie from a bread bag. "I like the new-wave look usually," he said. "It's kinda sexy, those girls with all the hair on one side chopped off? But this is a little hairy for a cook."

She wanted sympathy but didn't know what to say to get it.

"A fire, huh?" Carson said. "Is the place livable?"

"It's fine," she said, wishing she could hold out a charred hand as evidence of suffering. "It was like an apocalypse."

He laughed. "Maybe a minor apocalypse. I hope nothing *really* terrible ever happens to you."

She turned her back, threw a lump of margarine on the grill, winced when it sizzled. "What's your order, Carson?"

"I'm sorry," he said. "I didn't mean to be so offhand."

"It's okay," she said, shivering, glad to be wearing black. Sympathy had turned out to be the wrong response—now she wanted to cry.

"What's the entrée today?" Carson asked.

"Peanut butter and jelly," she said, seeing he wouldn't dare to cross her now. "White or wheat?"

"I hate peanut butter and jelly."

"Plain peanut butter it is, then." Meek, he wouldn't argue, and Kate softened. "So how's Annie?"

"She's okay, but I'm in guilt mode." Carson always argued

86

that tides of lust and guilt alternated, and that all change re-
sulted from this flow.

"Why?" Kate asked, putting turkey and lettuce on an onion
roll, his favorite.

"I'm not in love, I guess. I don't know." He smiled a hopeless little smile at her, and she returned it, touching his shoulder. This seemed to frighten him, but then the sandwich sat
quite solidly between them.

"You'll feel better when you get some sleep," he told her.

Sleep was not a possibility. Kate wore a flannel nightgown
and socks and long underwear to bed, then got up and put on
a sweater. She lay on her back, ready to jump at any noise; she
could close her eyes, but her muscles stayed wary. Every electrical outlet was suspect now.

"Carson," she whispered into the phone, "can you come over
here and talk to me? I know this building is going to burn down
tonight."

"Jesus, Katie," he said. She had known he would be in bed,
or almost in bed, with Annie. She could picture him lifting his
hand out of her hair to answer the phone. "That building is
brick, it can't burn down," he said.

Don and Terri left, slamming the door. The refrigerator was
making a new sound, a more metallic sound. Its cord was frayed
at the plug, and Kate imagined a flame running along the in-
sulation and blowing up the motor. She remembered seeing a
phone melted on a hot plate in college and wanted to drop the
receiver.

"Don said the wiring's shot all over the building."

"Annie's here," Carson said. "This is sort of an awkward moment."

"I've got a bottle of scotch," Kate said. "You two can drink
it all. You can bathe Annie in it if you want."

"Katie . . ." he said.

87

"I know we're not close enough for me to ask, Carson," she said. "I'm sorry."

They arrived with a plastic bag of triangular pills and sat at the bottom of the bed, leaning against the footboard, stretching their legs up so their feet nearly reached Kate's shoulders. Annie's fuzzy leg warmers and Carson's argyle socks with his checked trousers were comforting in themselves.

"The place smells of electricity," Kate told them.

"It's boiled cabbage," Carson said.

"For heaven's sake, Carson, it smells of pine needles," Annie said. "It's Christmassy. Did you get the wreath at The Posey Place? Maybe I made it." The wreath was flammable, and Kate hated the sight of it now.

Carson went to get a glass of water. "These will make you so sleepy you won't *care* if the building burns down," he said, holding out two pills. "Take one now and you'll be fine in twenty minutes."

Kate shook her head, wept pitifully into the quilt. She had to remain alert.

"Katie," he said, sitting down again, examining the pill as if he might decide to take it himself, "I know how you feel. It's a syndrome, a physiological thing. Some insects act like this for weeks at a time. They don't eat or sleep, they just watch." He made an intense, bug-eyed face as an example, then looked despairingly at Annie.

She was pretty, like a cat curled at the end of the bed, and sympathetic, saying she knew just how Kate felt, that she once fell two floors in an elevator and now always took the stairs. Kate cried at her kindness, sobbing into Carson's ankles. Looking up, she saw he was afraid Annie might misconstrue this, and she took a breath and sat back against her pillow.

Carson gave her relaxation exercises: she should tense all her muscles and then go limp. She couldn't do it.

"Listen," he said, "at least you're not like that diplomat

who suffocated under a pile of newspapers with his name in them."

"Carson," Annie said, "that's hardly reassuring."

"At least you didn't fall into a vegetable slicer and come out in lots of little cans."

"Carson has an odd sense of what might help," Annie said.

"Katie knows what I mean," he told her, hurt. "Katie's my dearest friend."

"Excuse me," Annie said. "I forgot Katie was your dearest friend."

Everyone was relieved when the phone rang. Carson jumped for it. "Carson's sporting goods, we love it when you play with our balls," he said. "Katie? Katie who?" He meant to tease her, but Kate couldn't play. She wanted safety and quiet, and she was afraid to touch the phone. Even when she realized it was Michael, she reached for it only because she knew Carson annoyed him, but Carson kept talking, asking about New York and music and whatever else came into his mind.

"Carson, let Kate have the phone and we'll go home and give her some privacy," Annie said.

"No, it's okay. I don't need privacy, really."

Annie settled glumly back. Carson sipped from her scotch, talking to Michael.

"Listen, let me ask you something," he said into the phone. "Suppose you were driving and you ran over a little animal. A rabbit. And this rabbit was dragging itself along just trying to find a place to die. Would you get out and kill it, or drive on?"

"God, Carson, give me the phone," Kate said.

"I don't know," Carson said to Michael. "You don't seem to me like the kind of guy who would bother to stop. You seem like you'd just let it suffer . . . Think of it all kind of soft and bedraggled . . ."

"Carson, you've got it *all* wrong. Give me the phone," Kate said. He did.

"What's going on there?" Michael asked.

"Nothing. I had a fire." She felt his hesitation. He was afraid she might need him. "It's okay," she said. "Nothing burned."

"So it's the middle of the night and Carson's there and he starts giving me a lecture on animal rights? I was just starting to write you a letter."

Carson was yelling, "The kind of guy who would drive away and tell himself he wasn't to blame!"

"What were you going to write in the letter?" Kate asked, though it was easy enough to guess: there'd be something pleading, something sad, and something angry, in sentences so disjointed Kate could read them differently each time.

"That's my bed you're in, you know," Michael said. "I bought it, if you remember."

"Well, you should come back here and sleep in it, then," Kate said, but without conviction. She had been careless with love, with everything, and in her minute of horror last night she had glimpsed a terrified death, alone.

When Michael didn't answer, she handed the receiver to Carson. "Hang up," she said.

He did. "That's my Katie," he said. "He's not good enough for you. I told Annie about him—I didn't think you'd mind."

" 'Course not, Carson," Kate said, though this meant Annie would see just an ordinary woe: Man Loses Interest, Can't Quite Leave.

"Yes, I'll sleep. I promise," Kate said. She turned out the light. Slipping into sleep would be a foolish loss of vigilance, but if she couldn't release Carson and Annie completely, she could at least let them get some rest. They lay together on the floor, under Kate's checked blanket. In bed, in the absolute dark, Kate kept rigid, listening with every nerve.

"You're afraid of being afraid, really," Carson said. "Just do the exercises one more time."

They spoke in unison: tense your feet; now relax them completely; now your legs; now your legs are completely relaxed. Kate smiled to think they really expected her to do these things. Still, as her eyes adjusted to the dark, the familiar shapes in the room comforted her. Dishes stood in the kitchen drainer; Michael's philodendron was drooping and she wondered what it needed—less water? more light? When Carson and Annie were quiet, falling asleep, she was relieved to concentrate only on the sounds, the possible dangers. The refrigerator went on, a car turned into the gravel driveway across the street. Then she heard something else, a kind of bubbling. She turned carefully toward it. Carson was kissing Annie.

"She's asleep, Carson," Annie whispered. "We can go."

"We can't," he said. "When she wakes up, she'll be terrified."

Silence of exasperation. Then: "Quit it, Carson."

"She's asleep," Carson said. "You said it yourself."

"*No*," Annie said, but she was laughing, and Carson prevailed. He moved to kiss her, to pull himself over her. The white checks of the blanket caught the light in varying patterns as the two moved beneath it, first slow and random, then in Carson's rhythm. It was like kinetic sculpture, Kate thought, dull but mesmerizing. Waking here with Michael, she used to find him watching her as if on the verge of discovery, deciphering the curves of her face. Bold, she would turn her open eyes to his, wanting him to know her. She couldn't imagine such yielding now. Watching the blanket rise and fall, she saw only that Annie was being held safe, away from harm.

"You're dreadful, Carson," Annie said then, sweet and sleepy.

"She's out like a light," Carson whispered. "Kate?"

She didn't answer, obliging.

"See?" he said.

"So, let's go home."

"She'd never forgive me," he told her.

"So what?" Annie said, aloud. "We've been here all night, Carson. This is *Vermont*. There are no lions or tigers or bears here."

"I'm awake," Kate said.

"And I'm leaving," Annie said.

"Annie, *Annie!*" Carson called her as she dressed, called down the hall after her, opened the window to call after her car.

"Go," Kate said. "Go ahead."

"You're sure?" He looked hopefully at her, but she shook her head no. "It's okay," he said, still watching out the window. "She'll understand."

Kate threw him his underwear, and he dressed awkwardly, coming back to sit on the bed. She sat up and hugged him, held him as tight as she could, her face buried in his neck, but his arms stayed at his sides. When she looked up, he was smiling his resigned smile, the one she always returned.

"What do you want for Christmas, Carson?" she said.

"You know I hate presents," he said. He squirmed, and she had to let go.

"Just tell me what you want."

"Nothing," he said, "and especially nothing over five dollars, because I can't spend more than five dollars on you."

"Carson, *what do you want for Christmas?* What?"

Carson always said that the only things he wanted besides a Nobel Prize were a little daughter to bounce on his knee, someone who would still love him when he was completely bald, and the knowledge that no woman could resist him. She wanted to give him these things at the very least.

"Please don't give me a Christmas present, Katie," he said. "I'm already in guilt mode. I just want to go to sleep."

"I can move over."

"The floor's fine," he said. "It's good for my back."

Leaving for work, Don slammed the door again. When no explosion followed, Kate took an even breath, but then the streetlight outside the window dimmed to lavender and flashed out, and every nerve flashed with it. It would take a while to get used to the knowledge that she was not safe, not even here. She'd been making a mental list of Christmas presents for Carson: Delson's had kaleidoscopes in the window—pairs of them, one that broke the world into thousands of bursting patterns and one full of its own fragments and designs. Watching him sleep, seeing the thinning spiral at the back of his head, she wished him a house with zinnias in the garden and a daughter in a party dress; also the power to dispel these things, to have a garden full of women follow him like the sun.

She punched Michael's number on the phone and listened to the empty ring in the distance, unsurprised.

"Who are you calling?" Carson was sitting up, confused. "Michael?"

"No answer," she said.

"Bastardo."

She nodded, smiling. "Do you want to call Annie?"

"No. I'll go by the flower shop later. It'll be okay. So what did you think?"

"Of Annie? Well, I didn't really catch her at the right moment. She's very pretty."

"I know," Carson said. "She's grouchy."

"It was an awkward situation," Kate said.

"No, she's just a grouch. But what a Twinkie, huh? But not really Ms. Right. Just Ms. Okay-for-the-Time-Being, I think. You're right."

"I didn't say anything."

"I always know what you're thinking, Katie."

"I'm thinking of switching to a full menu," she said. "Maybe I should stop feeding Chiverton according to my whims."

"Katie, if it weren't for your whims, I wouldn't know what to eat at all," he said. "Let's hold hands when we go downstairs—keep Terri on her toes."

He wanted to make amends, to smooth everything between them. The sun was up, spilling through the curtains, mocking her last night's fears. If Michael wasn't thinking of her now, Kate knew, he would be later, with guilt, even with longing. So she thought of him, an exhausted little blessing. The first time she met Carson, he'd come bopping into Buddy's, spun around on his stool, and asked her advice about a woman, someone named Jolene or JoAnne. Kate had told him to be patient, that love without difficulty could hardly be called love at all. When she told him about Michael, Carson had said she should leave him—why put up with such things?

Because there are only partial, shifting loves, and a world to be pieced from them.

"Of course, Carson," Kate said. "I'd love to hold your hand."

Audrey: Keeper of the Flame

Audie was with child. She sympathized, suddenly, with everything alive—tent caterpillars eating the trees, spider egg sacs hanging in the window casement. If she cleaned them out, it would be a jinx. Her mother called to give her advice, Pop was building a crib, but Steve didn't give a damn. In fact, he even said he didn't give a damn once, at midnight after a prepared-childbirth class. "Do you really think I give a damn?" he asked. He didn't mean the baby, he meant the class; but the class was for the baby.

He didn't care about the wood stoves either—he let Audie handle the situation. Everyone left Audie to handle the stoves.

Ma called her in the evening after Steve had left for work. "I've decided to settle this divorce myself," she said. "I'm going to take your father's stoves. That should be enough. I'll throw them down the stairs."

"How will you get them?" Audie asked. She was adding to a long list of names, girls on the right, boys on the left. *Hubert*, she wrote . . . *Bright in spirit.* "They're impossibly heavy."

"He can carry them up here on his back."

Penelope . . . *A weaver*, Audie wrote.

"I need a wood stove. I can't pay for oil and food on what he gives me."

"Do you need two wood stoves?" Audie asked.

"How much do you think he spent on those stoves? Hundreds of dollars. Thousands of dollars, but we couldn't get together the money to buy a new gas stove to cook on."

"What does the lawyer say, Ma?" Audie could feel the baby press its foot, or its elbow, out toward her side.

"I'll get them," Ma said. "It doesn't matter what the lawyer says."

Audie returned to her list. No one name seemed right for the child who was gently pressing out her boundaries as she sat staring at the page. The house was so quiet with Steve at work that she was startled each time the heat came up; the rush of warm air through the grate was too sudden, like a massive sigh. She wrapped an afghan around herself and tucked in the ends. When the phone rang again, she hated to uncover herself to answer it.

It was Pop. She sat down again with her list of names.

"She wants the stoves," he said.

"I know." She attempted sympathy. "What are you going to say?"

"She can have them," he said bitterly. "This thing has been going on too long. She'll trick me out of them somehow anyway. She said she'd give me the gold plates, so I gave her the rug, but now the plates aren't in any of my boxes and she swears she doesn't have them."

Nathan, Audie wrote in the boys' column . . . *Great gift.*

"Besides," Pop continued, "the stoves are in New Hampshire now. If she can get there to pick them up, she can have them. They're the last things we own. After this, there'll be nothing left to fight about."

"She'll get Steve to go pick them up." Audie could remember the vein standing out along Pop's arm as he tried to lift one of the stoves into the van, the day they brought them home.

Her father lowered his voice. "Ask him not to, Audie," he said.

"He'd love it," she told him. "It will get him out of prepared-childbirth class."

"Ma wants the wood stoves," she told Steve when he came in. "She says if he gives her the stoves, she'll stop asking for alimony."

"Well, that's a step in the right direction," Steve said. "Do you want a cigarette?" He lit one and threw the match into the fireplace.

"I can't. I'm pregnant."

"What does she need two wood stoves for?" Steve asked. "She doesn't want them for herself?"

"I don't know what she's going to do. She'll probably give them to us, like everything else of his. They'll take up the whole living room."

The room already held her father's oriental rug and every anniversary gift he'd given to Ma—the crystal pitcher was filled with straw flowers, and two antique clocks kept different times on opposite walls. Audie almost wished to have the stoves; if she kept all her parents' possessions, she might be able to make some order out of them.

They had brought the stoves home from an auction ten years ago, in early October. Audie went with Pop to keep him company. She had packed him a lunch: pieces of ham and cheese, the bread Ma had made the day before, eight apples. He loved apple pie, apple crisp, baked apples stuffed with raisins and brown sugar. He loved Ma's cooking best when Audie helped her. He said the apples she picked were the sweetest by far. The auction was five hours away, in the White Mountains, and Audie thought eight apples would be a good number for that long a drive. It was perfect weather, Audie's favorite weather—cool, with the leaves glowing against the gray sky. They sat on the van's high seats looking down the length of the valleys and up the heights of the hills. Classical music was on the radio—Audie would hear a Haydn sonata years later and recall suddenly a rocky brook flowing through a pasture, thinking it was something from a dream.

"If we can find a good wood stove," Pop said, "we'll have to lengthen the road." He had cut and stacked almost two cords of wood at the back door already—he wanted to heat the whole house with it. They were building a road up to the waterfall. Pop would find the best grade along the hillside behind the house and cut trees in a wide swath across it. They had been working on the road for five years, and Pop told Audie that when it was done, they'd build her a house at the end. When she was very young, she had believed this and thought she would live there as an adult, with her brother and sisters, growing her own food and swinging into the pool beneath the waterfall from a branch of one of the overhanging trees.

She sliced the apples carefully with Pop's pocketknife and handed him the slices one by one. When the radio station faded, they turned it off and sang. Neither was on key, but they made up in effort what they lacked in tune, and Pop agreed that the two of them were almost as loud as all six of the family. Audie got hoarse, though, and the sky got darker. They rode silently, watching the wind brush wet leaves up and over them. For miles they were the only car on the road.

A dirt road marked by a tiny auction sign ran off at the low point of a valley. On the left side was the remnant of a field, filled now with blackberry bushes. It was the first treeless space they had passed in miles.

"I'd enjoy living in this area," Pop said. "Plenty of room, no stray dogs running the deer. We'd only have to go into town every few weeks for supplies. Chucky and I would fish and hunt, and you girls would help your mother in the garden. We'd need a very big garden. You're safer out here than anyplace else— we'd have our own food, our own fuel, the family would be all together." The air seemed thinner to Audie—the mountains rose around them as steep as buildings, standing sharp against the sky. She wondered how many people would come so far for an auction.

Every folding chair was taken, though, when they arrived. Audie began to sort through a trunk full of old fabrics; a square of crimson silk disintegrated in her hand. The stoves, when she saw them, appeared softer than any cloth. The soapstone walls were like white flannel set in cast-iron lace. Pop drew his hand across the smooth surfaces, and the stone came off on his fingers like chalk. He started the bidding and kept his hand up as the other dreamers—even the wealthy men and the dealers— dropped out. Audie stood beside the stoves, as if she could shield them from a covetous glance, but she stepped aside when Pop turned to smile victoriously at her, and the stoves were so beautiful that she almost expected the auctiongoers to applaud.

"These stoves will keep us warm through the coldest winters," Pop said as they drove back along the empty highway. He reached across and pulled her braid. "Cozy, warm, and happy too."

It was the phrase Audie had used in her earliest childhood to explain well-being. Looking out through the corridors of the White Mountains then, from the high seat of the van, she could understand her father's vision; she saw that the radiated warmth would draw everyone in together and hold them there, closer to the flame.

The stoves did keep the house warm that winter. Too warm, Ma thought. She would come in and throw open the windows on the coldest night.

"How can you sit in this room?" she asked, pulling the pins

out and letting her hair fall. "You'll get terribly sick." It seemed awful, suddenly, to be sitting in such a warm room, playing cards together beside the stove.

"It's because you've just come inside, Lila," Pop said.

"Don't be ridiculous." She marched upstairs to take a shower.

Audie pushed open the bathroom door.

"Is that you?" Ma asked.

"Yes."

"I thought it was your father. How are you, sweetheart?"

"I'm good." Audie spread a towel over the radiator and sat down. The steam, permeated with Ma's soft perfume and plain soap, covered her glasses and the mirror. She had nothing to say. She cleared a patch of window and pressed against it to see the snowy hill behind the house. Pop's road up the hill was lit blue, but she could find no source.

"Is there a moon tonight?"

"It's almost full," Ma said. "Everything's sparkling outside." She stepped out of the shower and wrapped her hair in a towel. "It's so cold! Those stoves make the downstairs so hot it's impossible to breathe, and they leave it freezing up here." She used the wet towel to dry her legs, wrapped it under her arms, and turned out the light. "Come sit on my bed and we'll talk," she said.

Audie followed her down the hall. The big bed was covered with newspapers.

"Your father has managed to make twelve sections out of the Friday *Times*," Ma said.

Audie could see the moon from the bedroom window. It was as bright and small as a dime, and the land stood out as one cold plain in its light.

"Close the curtains, honey, and put this around you." Ma wrapped the extra quilt around Audie's shoulders and got into bed. "Why are you so quiet?" she asked.

"Just thinking," Audie said. Downstairs she could hear Pop

slam the stove door on another log. He was playing poker with Chucky and the girls. They laughed no matter who won the hand. "Let's make a plan," she said. She and Ma had always made plans together. They had planned how to live on a Caribbean island without any money, how Audie would go to a magnificent ball with a duke, how they would lay out the rooms in Audie's house by the waterfall when the road through the woods was built. "Let's plan my wedding."

"Again?" Ma laughed. "We've already planned it a thousand times, and you're not even fifteen." She was knitting a sweater of the deepest red wool. On the shelf behind her, stacks of shiny magazines were softened with dust. Photographs were propped up on them—of Audie's brother and sisters, her grandmothers and aunts. Some had tipped over, but the one of Audie stood sturdy in the light. She was sitting on the porch steps with two blond braids tied in red ribbons, smiling at the camera in absolute trust.

"I'll be married at home," she began, "in the winter. Katie and Grace will wear blue velvet dresses and I'll wear a white one, matching but fancier." The lamplight enclosed her with her mother and the photographs. She sat back against the wall and pulled the quilt tighter around her. "We'll decorate the whole house with white lilacs. We'll have them flown in from France."

She fell asleep at the end of the bed that night. Later, wakened by her father, she went downstairs to call in the dog. The stoves, standing in the dark of the living room, were two soft, lucid presences. Such cool firelight glowed through the white stone!

Audie did marry Steve in the winter, at Springfield City Hall. They went to the Motor Vehicle Department to have Audie's name changed on her driver's license, and to Steve's favorite restaurant for lunch, then home, to call Ma in Brimfield and

Pop in New York and Audie's sisters at work and her brother at school. Everyone was hurt, not to have been invited, but Ma had refused to come if Pop did, Pop had wanted to have the wedding in the church where he and Ma were married, and Audie had to call up everyone with compromises every other day, until finally white lilacs had seemed the dream of a foolish child.

"Steve, will you get me some ice cream?" Audie asked. He was looking over her shoulder at the list.

"Nathan!" he said, "Nathan? Penelope? Good old Audie, always prepared."

"What names do you like?" she asked.

"Luciano. Arabella."

"Arabella means spiderwoman," she said.

"Good. She can be a TV star."

"Butterscotch ripple? *Please?*" she said. "Isn't there any name you'd like the baby to have?" She illuminated the first letters of the names, causing the stems of the letters to blossom.

"All right, all right," Steve said, "but it's filthy in here. You know that."

The house *was* dirty. It needed vacuuming, and paint. The room for the baby had a broken window sealed over with cardboard. "Let's go buy wallpaper for the baby's room," she said.

"Audie, we've got three months. We don't have to jump up and do it now." He came behind her and kissed the top of her head. "Let's take a rest from this stuff. Let's go to the movies. We can't think about the baby all the time."

Abigail . . . My father is joy, she wrote. "Pop's going to let Ma have the stoves," she told him.

"She's the spiderwoman in your family, all right. But you take after her, Arabella."

"That's not funny, Steve," Audie said.

"Well, you have to admit she's running your father around in circles."

"He needs the exercise," Audie snapped. She poked his belly. "So do you."

"Don't push me, Audie. Look at your own waistline."

The cobwebs continued to collect, and with the warm weather came ants. Audie had heard that cucumber would repel them. She cut one into spears and left one on each cupboard shelf. She read cookbooks at work, whole cookbooks of reheatable meals for Steve's late dinners, and cookbooks of baby food. She bought seeds for her garden—beans and sunflowers and peppers and dill. She could picture herself spraying water over the crops with her infant on her hip, but she could not think, yet, of tearing up the weeds.

At home, opening the cupboards, she found her cucumbers writhing with glistening ants. Her project had failed, or succeeded. By the time she had all the ingredients for Italian chicken stewing in the slow cooker, it was dark. She took a peanut butter sandwich into the living room and turned on the lamp. In Steve's absence the house was filled with vague sounds: from the basement, from the attic, on the front porch. The dog crawled into the closet and whined. Even when she realized what the sound was, she wouldn't venture into the dark to coax him out. When Steve came home, he found her asleep on the sofa. He turned the bedroom light on and carried her upstairs to bed, where she rolled onto her back like a weighted clown toy, still asleep. The phone rang.

Audie could hear Steve answer. "Well, she's not *fast* asleep," he said. He held the receiver to her ear, and she wondered if it would be possible to sleep and listen at the same time.

"Can Steve go get the stoves for me?" Ma asked. "Your father will give me two hundred dollars to have them picked up, and then you can keep them. Will you ask him?"

"We don't need a stove, Ma," Audie said. Her list of names was still downstairs.

"Just ask him, Audie. I'm not asking anything of you."

"Okay, I'll ask.

"How is everything, honey? Did you get the baby's room all papered?"

Sleep slipped away. "We did," Audie said, "and Steve fixed the window and I'm making a little quilt for the crib. I'll appliqué a big red heart on it."

"Audie, you're going to be a wonderful mother," Ma said.

"I'm putting the phone on my stomach. Listen to the baby's heart." She pressed the receiver into her nightgown, and Ma swore she could hear.

Trying to sleep again, Audie planned the design for the quilt more intricately than before. She could picture the border of leaves and flowers carefully embroidered and the heart brilliantly red against the quilted ground.

In the morning their bedroom was reorganized by the light. The sheet lay over them like a landscape. Audie's belly was a sunny hill. Stretching, Steve broke the light and reached down to bring the dog up onto the bed.

"We'll go get the stoves, make two hundred dollars, and give them back to your father," he said.

"You'll be taking them under false pretenses."

"Not if I bring the stoves here before I give them back. If they're ours, we can give them to whoever we choose."

"If you go get those stoves, Steve, we're keeping them." Audie pulled a strand of her hair across her face and examined it in the light.

"Are you turning straw into gold, Rapunzel?"

"Don't mix your fairy tales. We have to get them straight before the baby comes." She heaved herself across the bed and sat on him.

He gasped. The dog yapped, grabbing Audie's exposed foot in his teeth. As she struggled to free herself, Steve turned her over and trapped her under him.

"Did you ever see a camel upside down?" he asked.

Audie whispered to the frantic dog, "Get him, Bonzo!"

The dog leapt over her back at Steve.

"You'll pay for this insolence!" Audie bellowed, rolling over. She had Steve locked between her legs, but couldn't sit up over her stomach to pull his hair.

Steve reached back and pulled Audie's arm, yanking her down toward the bed. They rolled together, hip over head, across the mattress. Audie felt the dog under her, squealing. She laughed, and could hear Steve laughing as they rolled, gathering Bonzo in undertow. When they came to the edge, Steve landed on his feet and Audie slid to the floor laughing, gasping, still fighting the sheet that came with her and the dog as he tumbled down over her head. The baby kicked furiously.

"If I have a breech birth, it's your fault," she said. "Poor Bonzo. Poor baby Bonzo."

Steve pulled her to her feet and kissed her.

"Charley horse!" she yelled, pinching his leg. He fell back onto the bed, and she went downstairs to slice cucumber for the ants.

Pop called her before she could start breakfast.

"How are you two going to make out financially after the baby is born?" he asked.

"Terribly," Audie said.

"We'll all be poor together," Pop said. "The lawyer is charging me twenty-five hundred dollars for court appearances alone."

"Oh, Pop, what are you going to do?" She didn't want to know. She lifted the flour canister carefully over a molested cucumber slice and started to mix batter for a coffee cake.

"Something always turns up," he said. "Is Steve getting the stoves for your mother?"

"I guess so."

"Well, he'll pick up a little extra money from that. And maybe I can help too."

Audie smashed the lumps out of the batter.

"How would you like to sell the stoves when you get them?" her father asked.

She poured the cake carefully into the pan. "What do you mean?"

"I'll pay you two hundred dollars apiece for them."

"Steve's probably not going to have time to go get them." Audie shook much too much cinnamon over the cake. She tried to pick it up with a damp paper towel.

"Well," Pop said, "will you consider it?"

"I've got something burning in the oven," she said. "I'll call you back. I love you."

"I love you too, sweetie," he said.

The stoves rested side by side in Audie's living room, disconnected, like men too old for battle. Audie sat beside them, wearing her nightgown. Still, she was too hot. The fan just blew hot air in at her. Her list of names had spread to a second page, and on the sheet facing it she was working out a budget—wood versus oil. The installation and the first cord of wood would easily use up four hundred dollars. She went back to the names. Steve had suggested one, finally. Wilfred, his grandfather's name. It was printed in his thick script at the bottom of the boys' column. Audie drew a slow line through the rest of the list. . . . *Desire for peace*, she wrote beside the baby's name. On the other side the names of the girls she might someday bear continued down the page. The stoves stood at the boundary of her circle of lamplight. Even the dog didn't venture past them. He ran around, barked at her and at the stoves, and bit her feet, so she pulled them under her with great effort.

The phone rang. She let it go on until Bonzo went crazy with it. She knew it was Pop.

"Did I wake you up?"

"No," she said. "I was in the shower. But I'm dry now."

"How's my grandson? All ready to be born?"

"He's really quiet. I think he's resting for both of us."

"How are the stoves?"

"They're here. Steve hasn't hooked them up yet."

"How much do you want for them?"

"I can't."

He laughed. "Even your mother would be pleased. She'll know she's soaked me twice."

"We're going to name the baby Wilfred," she said.

"Do you remember the day we bought the stoves?" he asked her.

"I do," she said.

"You were just a little girl. We had such a nice time that day, do you remember?"

"I do," she said. "But I was fourteen. And I'd like to give them back, but I can't." She could imagine the phone calls.

"Audie, I only gave them up because I trusted you."

Audie sat silent beside the stoves. Her foot was asleep. She couldn't seem to lift herself off it with the phone in her hand. The baby was still quiet. She pressed her hand into her stomach, willing it to move.

"Audie, are you there?"

"I'm here," she said.

"Audie, you don't have to tell your mother. You keep them for a while and give them back to me when she's forgotten. Do you remember the way we ran the pipes around the living room to radiate heat? And the time your mother cooked a whole dinner on the stove top for your birthday?"

Ma would have said she'd cooked dinner there because her

real stove didn't work. "I remember," Audie said. "I remember everything. I remember you and me and Ma and everyone cooking on the stoves, warming our feet against the stoves, cutting the wood for the stoves, but I can't make a deal like that. You gave them to her in the settlement. It was your decision."

"And she gave them to you. And they're mine," he said.

Finally the baby moved, kicked fiercely. The pain ran the length of her nerves.

"Pop, I don't want the stoves. They're in the way. They take up the whole room. I think I *will* sell them. Maybe you can buy them from whoever I sell them to."

"We built the road up to your house with the wood for those stoves," he said.

She stood up. "My house. My house? Where is my house? Give me back the road to my house and I'll give you back the stoves! Okay? They're your stoves, they're Ma's stoves, they're my stoves now! They'll probably burn the house down. But I can't give them back to you. Ma would hate me!" She crumpled her list of names and threw it at one of the stoves. Bonzo went yapping after it.

"Pop," she said, "no one's going to cook on them now."

"I'll cook for Wilfred," he said.

Wilfred caused her another deep cramp.

"I love you, Pop."

"I'll come get them next weekend," Pop said. "Steve can help me."

"Okay," Audie said. "I'll call you tomorrow."

"I'll call you," he said.

She pressed the button and dialed her mother.

"Ma," she said, "I just blasted Pop and it's not fair unless I yell at you too. I'm sick of it. I'm selling the stoves back to him. I know you'll hate me but I don't care. Everyone will hate me anyway. You're telling me what to do, he's telling me what to do, and I don't know what to do. And don't tell me I'm taking Pop's side. I just want to be home with Steve and Wilfred and bake bread and try to live. I don't have room for the stoves!"

"Who's Wilfred?" Ma asked.

Audie could feel it again. The pain was exactly what they had described in the classes. "What does it feel like to be in labor?" she asked.

"If you have to ask, you'd better call Steve," Ma said. "I'll meet you at the hospital. And don't worry, Audie," her voice was perfectly, powerfully calm. "You have plenty of time."

Bonzo leapt up from sleep and attacked Audie's leg.

"Lie down," she told him.

She dialed. "Steve, Ma thinks I'm in labor. Will you come get me?"

"I'm on my way," he said.

"Don't worry, we have plenty of time."

She rose, squeezed between the stoves. Bonzo followed her up the stairs. Each footfall echoed upward, but the house was full of the first summer air, and she heard none of the usual unsettling sounds. She turned on the light in the baby's room. She had swept and dusted that morning, so everything was in order. The quilt with the heart appliqué rested smoothly over the crib mattress. In the rocking chair Pop's old teddy bear sat forlorn. A ladybug crawled along one of the stripes in the wallpaper, and Audie let it continue along her hand. She opened the window. Across the street houses were still lighted and a woman stood on her front steps, calling a dog. Audie reached out and shook the ladybug into the cooler air.

Elysian View

If only we could know the future, we wouldn't so much mind death, but as it is, we are waiting for the morning mail. Every lady at The Elysian View Home died with a lottery ticket in her purse. The living stayed on in hope of victory at the next bridge game, or an extra piece of cake for dessert. Lila Vanderwald was Director of Recreation at Elysian, responsible for arts, crafts, and cocktails, wheelchair aerobics and the annual Mother-Son Ball. It was the only job she could find after the divorce. If she hadn't poured the first half of her life down the drain of her marriage, she could have been an international banker by now, or a federal judge; a citizen of marble hallways, wealthy, important, in charge. Instead, skirt hitched, she was kneeling on her office rug to cut paper palm trees for the upcoming "Evening at the Folies Bergère," a clump of silver glitter glued by mistake in her silver hair. She was fifty-two. Possibility seemed to be closing against her. She saw she was going to die wishing, for the same things she had wanted all her life.

These bitter thoughts twisted again at the sight of Jean Brenehan, former Sister of Mercy, now Chief Administrator. Lila sat back on her haunches and blinked. Jean B. remained sanctimonious even beneath false eyelashes and décolletage: her much-uplifted bosom quivered with disapproval now, for no reason Lila could guess. Her face, Lila thought, revealed how few and how small were the thoughts that passed behind it, all of them suitable to be jotted on the clipboard she held at her side.

"Frank Gunn is dying," Jean B. said, smartly. Room 115 would be free.

"I'll go up," Lila said, meaning to show that some people cared more for the man dying than for his empty bed. She groaned as she stood, not so much from exertion as dramatic habit: she gave a little extra emphasis to each act until her life seemed as large as it should have been, with many tragedies and comedies each day. When it came time for Lila's raise, though, Jean B. would remember the groan and say she wasn't agile enough, or was too loud.

Even crying was forbidden: it only added to the general hysteria and confused the bereaved. If Jean B. was all rules, Lila was all transgressions, and she wept now with both grief and spite. She knew little of Frank Gunn, save that he drank, was said to be lecherous, and had once told a woman at a party she was the ugliest woman he'd ever seen. He had gone grim and gray with disappointment long before he was old, but Lila was sure she had seen into his fierce heart. When he first came to Elysian, he had scribbled a poem on a napkin and held it out for her to read, his face hopeful that one time. But the letters bled to blots, and she tried vainly to decipher them while he smiled up at her, awaiting her reaction. Finally she laughed and bent to ask him what he had written, but his dignity was offended and he turned away. Since then she had taken every opportunity to admire him, but he dismissed her. Now he was dying, still unpraised.

The pietà in Room 115 stanched tears. Mary Gunn was fumbling through her husband's IV tubes, trying to hold him, touched by the same shaft of sunlight that crossed the dead man's knees. Peevish Mary, usually prepared to take offense wherever offense might offer, was speaking in a high, gentle voice, as if reassuring a child.

"Oh, Mrs. Gunn . . ." Lila rushed halfway across the room toward her before remembering that only the head nurse was supposed to attend a death.

Mary started, regained herself. "Come in," she said dryly, "there's nothing to be afraid of." Her hair was braided and wound Valkyrie-style, her eyebrows shaven, replaced with a fiercer, painted pair. Mary Gunn dealt in matters of fact, or tried to. She allowed an embrace but straightened her collar the minute Lila let her go.

Lila wanted to say that she was afraid of Jean B., not death, but Mary had unzipped her purse and was rooting among the cigarette packs and pill bottles there, all business. She found a small, battered notebook, wet her thumb, and flipped to the page marked "Funeral."

"Mr. McHoul from the funeral home is on his way," she said. "The service is to be Saturday, at St. Paul's. We're not God-fearing people"—she gave a small, ironic smile—"but these old New England churches are as light as the Italian. We were married in Florence, you know."

"No," Lila said, "no, I didn't." The thought of that wedding and its vain attendant hope so tightened her throat that she dared not go on.

"Well, no matter." Mary flipped a page, as if to hurry on to the next detail, then looked away, over the lands given by the Elysian family for the nursing home. The slope had been an overgrown orchard once, but it was pruned to miniature perfection now, studded with ornamental shrubs. Two maples had been left standing, streaming yellow leaves over the pond.

Mary gathered Frank's comb and tube of salve. "One thing," she said, "he didn't *say* a word. You hear of the final summoning of strength and what-have-you, but in fact he just died, just as you'd expect."

Had Mary been expecting a last endearment? "They rarely speak," Lila lied, thinking of Lettie Willward, who had sat bolt upright, uttered a neat, satisfied "Grand slam," and subsided as if deflating, never to take a trick again. And Mr. Oliver, whose wife had died only a month before him, had cried, "There you are!"

"Mr. Gunn was such a good man," Lila said, feeling this in every bone, only because she was sure Mary would want to hear it. "Everyone will miss him."

"Yes," Mary said, "we'll need to run a bus to the funeral."

She was serious, Lila realized, in time to convert giggle to cough.

"Well, a van at the least," Mary said. She gestured toward the window, where at the base of the long hill St. Paul's steeple rose like a sugar cake decoration. "It's nearly a mile. And remember the traffic when the Admiral died." Admiral and Edith Fickett had stood at the center of town society. Lila had nearly fainted in the crush at that funeral, but Frank Gunn, failed poet, was not likely to draw a crowd. However, she promised to arrange transportation, and at the thought of stalwart Mary harboring so fragile a wish, she burst into tears again.

"Don't, dear," Mary said, giving her a couple of stern pats. "Well," Lila thought, "who but a fool wouldn't cry?" She would cry until Thornhill River ran salt if she felt like it, if Frank Gunn could die without admiration, without speaking to his wife. If she, Lila Vanderwald, was meant to have lived without love, without making even the smallest mark.

"I'm sorry," she wept, face in her hands. Leaving, she turned to repeat the apology, but Mary had forgotten her. She had taken the sheet in her two hands to pull it over Frank's face, but instead she sat and put her ear to his chest.

At the nurses' station the oldest ladies were set out like so many houseplants in the society of the hall. They leaned in as Lila passed, and called to her: Lila, Lila, like a soft wind.

Rheumy-eyed, fumbling, they needed her and couldn't see the tears. She bent to each of them, close enough so they could see her smile and smell her cologne.

"You were the best dancer, Lila," said Minna Wence, who had lost the knack of the present altogether. Lila imagined, in spite of herself, the fresh-cut lawn bordered with mock orange, her feet bare in the grass, her dress whirling out behind. The ladies of Elysian View remembered well the parties given by the Admiral and Edith Fickett at Broadlawns, once the imperial palace of Main Street, broken into condominiums now. Beside the starry-eyed Minna sat Edith herself. Commanding even from her wheelchair, she lifted her lorgnette and looked up at Lila very much as if she were actually looking down.

"Have you been *crying?*" she asked. How, Lila wondered, did such a curved and shrunken person contain so strong a voice? The collar of Edith's lace robe reached her ears, and the hem hung long as a christening gown. Within lived a woman who in her most difficult hours had needed only to consult Emily Post, and who had carried the authority of this text with her through the years.

"Frank Gunn died," Lila said, with a great sniff. She re-called, though, that Edith had not cried even at the Admiral's funeral, but had stood shaking every hand, accepting tribute, holding the light as Lila had seen the river do after the sun was down.

Edith would never fail to show proper sympathy, though she remembered only vaguely, and with a vague distaste, who Frank Gunn was. "Oh, my dear," she said, letting the lorgnette hang. "He was such a good man." If she could not recall why she disliked him, here she was proven right: death looked like a failure of dignity to Edith Fickett, just the sort of thing one might expect of Frank Gunn. She had learned to speak only good, though; it wasn't hard to imply the rest.

"So sad," she said, "he was a communist, I believe." But she didn't know Lila's politics. "Those communists must have been so *brave*," she added. "Now he's gone to a better place." How could there be a better place? Well, this sort of thought was best suppressed.

"Say," she said, hurrying on, "Lila, have you seen the Admiral this afternoon?"

Edith allowed no contradiction, but policy insisted that Lila remind her: the Admiral was dead.

"Oh, Mrs. Fickett," she said, pleading, "you know . . ." but Edith had raised the lorgnette again. Lila took a deep breath. "Admiral Fickett is dead. You know that."

"Of course I know that, Lila, but he hasn't come home to lunch."

True enough. "I'll check the billiard room," Lila said.

"Oh, no, he doesn't approve of billiards."

"I'll try the tennis court," Lila said. She headed in a direction that might, if there had been tennis courts, have led to one.

"Thank you, dear." Edith folded her hands and turned to Minna Wence, who was still dreaming of waltzes past and asked what the theme of the next Broadlawns dance was to be.

Edith kept her lap full of notes, reminding herself of appointments and chores, but, sifting them now, she saw no plans for a party. "Honestly," she confided to Minna, "these days there seems to be nothing on my mind but my hair." Had she sent the invitations and forgotten the party? She forced a gay laugh. "I haven't decided," she said.

When Mary Gunn came along, carrying an exhausted, grief-struck silence only a shade deeper than her usual, Edith remembered the conversation with Lila and was prepared. "He was such a courageous man," she said. She would not, of course, speak ill of the dead, nor think it, but unfortunately this left her at a loss for words. "When is his funeral, dear?" she asked. "Here, will you write it down for me?"

Saturday, October 19, Van Leaves at 9:30, South Portico, Mary wrote.

"Thank you, dear," Edith said, and filed it beneath "Manicure, Tuesday P.M."

TODAY IS MONDAY, OCTOBER 21
THE NEXT MEAL IS: LUNCH

The signboard at the nurses' station was meant to give everyone a leg up on reality. Edith, studying it, finally decided to make a note. *Lunch,* she wrote on the back of an envelope from one of those dear old oil companies her husband had loved. "Important," the envelope read. "Proxy material enclosed."

Important. Edith took it in her lap to the window, as she had taken Isaac's letters to the field to read them, when they were engaged. She would wade in among the red and yellow hawkweed, hitching her skirts to take the sun on her legs. She smiled. She was nostalgic for all life now, every detail. How well her imagination had served her, back then, reading love between Isaac's lines on pump repair and shipboard meals!

"Do you know," she said to Lila, who had just come with the sherry for the bridge game, "I don't believe I've *ever* seen such a beautiful fall."

Lila agreed, but Mary Gunn, who had been keeping nervous vigil since Frank's funeral on Saturday, waiting to see Lila, came up behind them to say she could see no beauty in anything so slothfully tended. The topiary seemed to shrink as she spoke. "Can I speak to you in your office?" she asked Lila, in an ominous undertone.

As soon as she delivered the sherry, Lila said, and went off with a sigh, feeling properly chastised for taking pleasure where there was none to be had.

Courteous, Edith thought, Mary Gunn had never been. Imagine speaking so cruelly of that field, where they had all

116

gathered raspberries as children. But Mary was in mourning; she must be forgiven.

"How are you feeling dear?" Edith asked.

"Fine, thank you. Fine," Mary said. "One learns to handle these things."

One does? Edith wondered if she had mistaken the subject.

"The service was lovely, though," Mary added, with a fearsome emphasis that caused Edith to touch her notes, though she dared not look down in case one marked "Funeral" should appear on top.

"I was so sorry to have missed it," Edith said, considering various excuses before falling back on her usual "It's this damn chair." (She did not speak the word "damn," of course, only mouthed it.) "There's never a ride available."

"There was supposed to be a van."

"Oh," said Edith, covering her notes with her hands, "oh, no, I don't think . . ."

"Perhaps there was an administrative error," Mary said. "Lila was supposed to arrange a van."

"Exactly. An administrative error," Edith said, so relieved she felt a surge of warmth toward Mary. "There was no van, I'm sure," she said, "and it's such a shame, dear. I *so* wanted to go. I'm sure it was grand," she said, heading off toward the bridge game, the wheelchair in drive. "Next time, absolutely," she called over her shoulder. Then she was aghast. Hadn't they been discussing a funeral? It couldn't be.

"Tra-*la*, tra-la-la-la," she sang, softly, absently. It was the most rousing phrase of "The Marseillaise," which she had used to sing to herself just before she descended the staircase into the midst of a fête, her fine blond hair piled high. She had always felt triumph was at hand when she heard those notes: now they carried the faux pas out of her mind. She was sure, suddenly, that the cards would fall for her today.

Next time? Mary heaved her purse onto Lila's desk and took

a seat. "There seems to have been an administrative error," she said, resting her cigarette in the ashtray in order to look Lila straight in the eye. "There was no transportation to Frank's funeral." Her voice thinned and threatened to fail. "Edith Fickett was unable to go to the church."

This, Lila saw, was the saddest thing in the world, the trifle that condenses a life of pain to a single, lethal drop. Brucie, who drove the van, had said there were no riders: funerals were far too common at Elysian to attract much attention, and Saturday had been blustery, and the Reverend Sleight was rumored to believe in Hell.

"There's no need to apologize," Mary said. Lila had intended no apology, but she was ever willing. Mary's sorrows, her joyless smile which served only to confirm the fitness of everything wrong, could not be helped, but it was crucial, awful, that her plans had gone awry.

"I'm so sorry . . ." Lila began.

"Please." Mary held up a hand. "These ceremonies." She blew out a great smoky breath and lit a new cigarette. ". . . but they are important to some people . . . you should have heard Edith just now, she was devastated."

That wicked old dissembler could not be devastated by a freight train, thought Lila, pulling a sympathetic face.

"I think it would be best if we played a tape of the funeral," Mary said, "for those who were unable to attend."

"There's a tape?" All life looked bizarre to Lila—the crucifix swinging between Jean B.'s breasts, the nurses' aides running through their cancan for the Folies Bergère—but this, she was sure, taxed propriety's limit.

Mary pulled her purse into her lap and rummaged. There it was, a purse-sized tape player and miniature cassette. "You see," she said, "I just held it in my lap, with the prayer book. I wonder you don't use one of these in your work, Lila. The sound quality is remarkable." She pressed a button, and the machine issued an unearthly fugue.

"We can reserve one of the sitting rooms for tomorrow night, serve . . . sherry, and a few small cakes, and there should be a simple flower arrangement, nothing ostentatious . . ."

Without ostentation, who would want to attend? But Mary was all animation, now they had a plan. She lit a new cigarette, though one was still burning down in the ashtray, and flipped through her notebook to start a new page.

Lila clasped her hands on the desktop and spoke as teacher to student, or mother to child. "It is unusual . . ." she began.

Mary had evidently been waiting for this; she sprang.

"Unusual," she said, and began a lecture that was to cover the spread of fascism and the rise of an anti-intellectual elite before reaching the sturdy declaration that she and Frank had never trod upon the ordinary paths, though of course if Lila . . .

"Forgive me," Lila said, "you are absolutely right."

"You don't have to give in," Mary said, no less sharply. Frank would never have given in, Lila thought. They must have been like two dogs with an old sock.

"I want to give in," Lila said. From the absurd she had risen, to the absurd she was doomed to return.

When Mary, having issued a few more directives, left, Lila pulled a sheet of oaktag from her drawer and drew a thick black border around it.

Frank Gunn, she wrote. *Selections from His Funeral.* This didn't look very inviting, so she added *Refreshments* in violet below.

"Look, you have a second chance," she said to Edith Fickett as she pinned up the sign. "Frank Gunn's funeral again tomorrow."

Edith was too well bred ever to show surprise. "Oh, lovely," she said softly to herself as she searched for her notepad. "Lovely,

lovely, lovely, hooray, hooray, hooray." With not a trace of irony, so Lila saw she had put it out of her mind.

"Tomorrow," Lila said again.

"Tomorrow," Edith echoed.

"*Write it down,*" Lila said. *Tomorrow,* Edith wrote, with two underlines.

"And you are really planning to go, aren't you?" Lila asked.

"You are *so nervous,* dear," Edith said. "It hurts me to see you overwrought. The things of this world aren't so important as all that, you know. And *don't* make such a face, Lila, you'll cover yourself with wrinkles, and around those *beautiful* blue eyes . . ."

On she went, while Lila imagined a quick and tidy strangulation, carried out with the lorgnette chain. A mannerly, elegant death.

"Lila, this is extremely unusual." The chill in Jean B.'s voice froze everyone in the room. The nurses' aides, rehearsing, let their skirts fall and stood like girls under a dancing-master's rebuke. Jean B., holding out the funeral poster, was all atremble. She saw danger in every mystery, and few things were not mysterious to her.

"Is it some kind of a . . . a . . . a joke?" she asked. Lila's heart went out to her, by accident. She sounded so afraid.

"Mrs. Gunn wanted to play a tape of Mr. Gunn's funeral, for the shut-ins," she said, with enough gravity that Jean B. returned to her notes.

"Well, it doesn't come under Recreation," Jean B. said, finally. "There's no policy on this."

"I know." A tiny smile crept over Lila's face. She couldn't help it.

"I have had enough of your insolence," Jean B. snapped.

Lila remembered, suddenly, the ruler over the knuckles: the awful surprise of pain and the other children looking down, as the aides in their pink costumes did now. To be spoken to so, and by a woman as shallow, as pitiable, as Jean B.! Everything a failure, all her plans unaccomplished, the efforts of affection wasted, the daily toil to produce . . . prettily wrapped bridge prizes and inspiring bulletin boards.

Jean B. held up the sign, as if to rip it, but she must have seemed foolish even to herself for a moment. "It's not to happen again," she said, smacking the sign down on the table and hurrying out.

But it would, Lila thought, if she liked. It would happen again and again until The Elysian View Home was nothing but a three-ring funeral, with herself bespangled in its midst.

She had wished for many things before: a thriving love, a secure future, an important job, but finally, something was to be granted. Frank Gunn's soul could not rest, it seemed, without Edith Fickett's benediction, and Edith, at the mere mention of death, felt the time was right to make order from chaos in her top bureau drawer.

"Important," Edith said, taking out the letter she had received the day before, turning it over in wonder. The Admiral had always managed their money, so now it was her job to keep the important things together, in the top drawer, for the man from the bank. She took out everything with a dollar sign or number and piled it on the bed. When she came to her note, "Tomorrow," she felt a little thrill, wondering what was to happen tomorrow. Was it a holiday? Was there an Indian summer picnic planned? Of all picnics she loved an Indian summer picnic best. Whatever it was, it was important, and she set the note in the Important pile, efficient and pleased.

Tomorrow had come, in fact, and nearly gone. In the Admiral Isaac Fickett Memorial Sitting Room, Lila had arranged six armchairs in séance position. Most of the furniture at Elysian had been donated, and Mary Gunn's tape player sat like a sacred scarab on the round table Edith's grandfather had brought back from India in the *Bright Prospect*, his clipper ship. Mary carried two pots of mums from windowsill to table, waiting for the mourners, then back to the window again. The dinner hour was ending, the hour of Frank's service had come. She heard snatches of aimless, companionable chatter as the residents turned into their rooms. No one came to her door. She returned to the window, watching couples who lived as she and Frank had, in cottages on the grounds, pass beneath her toward their lighted homes. When she went to the door again, she saw no one in the hall.

Seeing the note "Tomorrow" on top of the pile she had just made, Edith had a foreboding and considered several disagreeable obligations, never thinking of Frank Gunn. Well, better not to worry . . . The last item in her top drawer was a cocktail napkin from the *Queen Mary*, with a perfect lipstick imprint. Oh, those dear old ships, where she and Isaac had reclined in the palm of each other's affection . . . (Isaac had been cranky, ill at ease as a passenger, but never mind.) The sun rose, it seemed, solely to warm them, the sea moved solely to rock them, and here was her only souvenir. She added it to the Important pile, which she wrapped in Saran Wrap left from a breakfast in bed, and tied with red ribbon, for importance. A good evening's work, and she was looking forward to tomorrow again, without remembering why.

Mary Gunn heard a step in the hallway and stood to receive her guests. There was only Minna Wence, making slow progress in her walker but smiling enormously, with a great red bow in her hair.

"Thank you," Mary said, with injured gravity, shaking Minna's hand. "He would be so glad to see you."

"I wouldn't miss it for the world, dear," Minna said. "Will there be dancing?"

———

Important, Lila wrote, in scarlet, on a sheet of oaktag so large she had to spread it on the floor. ("What's needed," Mary had explained, "is a larger sign. Edith couldn't see it from the wheelchair. She was terribly disappointed.") *Frank Gunn's Funeral Will Be Replayed at 6 P.M. Wednesday Evening. Attendance Is Mandatory.* Lila sucked on her pen a moment and decided to throw caution to the winds. *This Means You*, she added, then gathered caution back to herself and illuminated the letters until they became lilies, one by one. "If it makes Mary happy," she thought as she worked, knowing full well that she would not make Mary happy and must continue to try.

When time came to face Jean B., Lila found her strength in the hand mirror, in her own silver-blue eyes. Edith's flattery might be ungenuine, but it was not in fact untrue. Lila held the mirror closer until she could see only her eyes, the old beauty of determination unchanged though the flesh had slackened over it. Until Edith spoke, Lila had forgotten what she could draw from her own image. She shut the mirror in the desk drawer and went to face Jean B.

"Mrs. Fickett has asked that we hold another service," she explained. The Ficketts' only daughter had committed suicide years ago, so their fortune would now go to Elysian View.

"Very good," said Jean B. Her phone rang, and Lila could hear in the new warmth of her voice that it was a man. A prosthetics salesman, from the conversation. Jean B. had left the convent in search of a more worldly love but had found none. Past forty now, with only the dream of romance, never the old soupbone love, she toyed with her crucifix and tossed her hair, and Lila had to turn away.

"Lila, Lila, a snake!" Minna Wence was reared up in her chair, watching a National Geographic special on the nurses' station TV. The snakes did look real, taunting the camera, loll-

ing out of the trees. Cheerful Nurse Carp explained from behind the desk that it was only the television, nothing to fear.

Lila took two quick steps and lifted the spectral snake from
the old woman's lap, turning her arm so it could be imagined
to wind upward, even to shoot its quick tongue. She held it
out to Nurse Carp, who shrank at first, though finally she accepted it and carried it away behind the desk.

"Thank you," said Mrs. Wence, smoothing her robe, then
her hair. When she touched the bow over the bald spot, her
thoughts returned happily to things satin.

"Will you be at Broadlawns tomorrow, Lila?" she asked. Lila
wished she had been born into the right age or class to have
been at Broadlawns once. She pictured a brigade of florists,
passing fuchsias like fire buckets up the wide stairs. She leaned
against a chair and spoke as from delicious indecision.

"I don't know . . . I just can't make up my mind."

"What I was wondering . . ." Mrs. Wence hesitated, as if
about to ask a great favor, then plunged ahead. "Would you
. . . could I . . . borrow the gold chiffon?"

The gold chiffon? From the look on Mrs. Wence's face, Lila
could almost conjure herself young and fair in a gold chiffon
cloud. "Oh, it would look wonderful on you," she said. "Of
course you can wear it. I have a new one, cut very low."

The old woman's face lit like a girl's. "Tell me all about
it, dear." Lila gave her a boost into her walker and kept lin-
gering pace along the hall, describing clouds of silk the bound
less blue of the evening sky. It was the morning of the third funeral, and as she talked she ticked off her responsibilities in her
mind.

". . . and a wide, soft sash that almost touches the ground,"
she said, as they turned at Mrs. Wence's door. She had forgotten for a moment that she was inventing the dress, and began
to worry about matching shoes.

"Oh, Lila, it will be grand." Mrs. Wence dropped into the

chair Lila pulled out for her, with a soft smack like a fly ball into a fielder's mitt. "I'm so tired of my white, even if it did come from Paris." She gestured toward the closet. Lila stepped in, between the Floridian polyesters and Irish cardigans redolent of Bal à Versailles.

"This one?" she asked. It was a white silk sheath, slit as high as any man would dare hope, beaded from nape to knee.

"Oh, my dear," Mrs. Wence said, clapping her hands together. "Oh, try it on."

Lila was sure she could shrink or swell to fit anything beautiful, but once she had shimmied in, she despaired of escape. "Oh," Mrs. Wence said, soft and reverent. In the mirror Lila saw herself truly: pale and tall as a marble Athena. At a quarter to six, still unsure she could ever remove the dress, she carried a tray of pink and green cakes the length of the main hall, easily drawing attention from the TV.

"For the *bereaved*," she said to the ladies assembled. "*After the service.*"

Mrs. Wence, stalled in her walker, broke into a stricken, yearning smile and peered toward the confectionary until Lila had to offer an arm, so that both of them lost balance, grabbing blindly at the walker and bracing for a rain of cakes. The tray teetered overhead, shifting now toward the window and the setting sun, now eastward again, until, through a feat of perfect attention, a momentary forgetting of all but the cakes aloft, the women kept them there, and themselves upright as well.

"Is there a party?" Mrs. Wence gasped.

"Shall we go in together?" Lila said.

Though she had filled the room with white lilies, Lila could do little to lighten the aspect of Mary Gunn, who stood wringing her hands in the doorway, looking about as if, though prepared to resent anything, she could find nothing out of place. But here was Lila, in her white dress. Mary turned her head and offered her hand only to Minna Wence.

"Thank you," she said pointedly. "It means more than I can say."

"I see," said Mrs. Wence, betrayed. Mary Gunn was not welcoming her to Broadlawns. She turned from Lila, too.

The four or five others who had followed were confused only for a moment, then they followed the impulse in the organ prelude and sat solemnly down. When, after a few minutes, a spring of gay chatter erupted, Mary lifted her handkerchief to stifle it.

"Was the sign too high for wheelchairs?" she asked Lila, not meeting her eye. "I don't see Edith."

"I'll check her room," Lila said. It was empty. Then Lila heard a faint tra-la. Edith Fickett was abroad, though heading the wrong way.

"You shouldn't be humming, Mrs. Fickett," Lila said, seizing the wheelchair handles from behind, "you're on your way to a funeral."

"I . . . what?" Edith said, but regained herself. "Not humming, dear," she said. "Humming is an aimless and vulgar pursuit . . ." But they were turning, they were on their way in.

"Edith," Mary said, "how kind."

For one long, terrible moment, Edith groped and found nothing, not her name or her home or any of the beliefs that had drawn her through life. Then she closed her hand on the firmest thing she knew: she must always, always be polite.

"I'm honored to be asked," she said. Though she could not remember Mary's name, she knew, seeing her face, what to say: "I'm so terribly sorry." And saying it, she felt it; sorry for Mary's loss which none of them could measure, for the leaves drifting away from the trees, for herself and her old dreams.

Mary nodded, clasping her hands, waiting for Edith to go on. "Lila," Edith asked, "did you know . . . him?"

"Mr. Gunn?" Lila asked, giving Edith a clue. "We only spoke

a few times." She hated to mention speech, reminding Mary of Frank's tight-lipped death.

"What a shame," Edith said, ad-libbing, talking on faith. All sorrows were similar, weren't they? No love satisfied, none was complete enough to crush and comfort its object. "He was so reserved, you know," she said, "but how he loved our Mary here." The name had leapt to mind as a gift; Edith was profoundly grateful. "And how he admired you, my dear, it showed in his every word and deed."

"Thank you," Mary said, as if acknowledging the most perfunctory condolence, but then she looked down and said again, "Thank you," humbly, to herself alone. The organ music fell away, and after a muffled thump and crackle the Reverend Sleight took up his funerary drone.

Mary came to the back of the room and said to Lila, very softly, "Perhaps we can keep the tape on file for anyone who'd like to run through it again."

"A wonderful idea," said Lila, pouring a glass of sherry. Mary accepted it, while the others bowed their heads, listening to the Reverend Sleight go on.

Lila raised her own glass. If she had not provided the funeral of Mary's dreams, if her event had not the mighty solemnity of the imagined ideal, still it had a luster: the plastic cups of sherry glistened, the lilies lifted their fragile heads, Lila's dress took the light like a prism. This event was at least her own.

"To Frank," she whispered, touching Mary's glass with hers. Then another toast, in thanks, to the God she could never quite believe in. Surely, deep at the center of the moral universe there turned a beautiful star. Lila leaned back against the refreshment table but stood again, lest the dress split a seam.

The moon was rising, just a day on the wane, and the puny trees grew sharp against a fathomless sky. Edith, who had heard the Episcopal funeral service often enough to have memorized it, saw she had missed the full moon. Why had she not gone to the window last night? She would have to wait another month now, into November, and she considered, with the iron calm she had practiced against the inevitable, that no one could promise her another month. How could she have forgotten the harvest moon? Her hands closed on the armrests with a strength that surprised her. How could anyone ask her to sit here while the moon rose up beyond the view from the window, perhaps for the last time?

"Lila," she said, in her fullest, haughtiest Yankee tone, so loudly she drowned out the ashes-to-ashes-and-dust-to-dust, "it's time to go now. It's getting dark as a pocket in here."

We Face Death

When Ma had nowhere to go, after her divorce, Abe Withan
let her move into his chauffeur's quarters—the Withans only
keep a gardener and one hired hand. It was a low, vine-covered
cottage attached to the garage, across the driveway from the big
house. The rooms were dark and narrow and always smelled of
the damp, but from the backyard Ma could look out over the
Withans' vegetable garden, their orchard on its long march
toward the valley, then the roofs and spires of Brimfield amid
the southern hills. When she pulled a beet in that garden, it
was as if she could hold it up for the whole world to see. She
was only supposed to stay at the Withans' a few months, until
she found a job and got back on her feet, but she could never
bring herself to leave. It's been seven years now, and my sisters—Grace and Audie—and I have come to think of that
house as our home. The day I finally gave up on Lawrence I
drove straight there.

I'd spent all night packing, all day in the car, my head spin-
ning with accusations and entreaties. I set my hand on Ma's
latch with a pilgrim's weary joy, imagining a cup of tea, but I
opened the door to a blast of heat and laughter.

Ma was standing like a diva before her whole salon.

"How can you laugh at me?" she asked them, laughing herself, wiping her eyes. "I'm telling you, it was terribly sad!"

Abe's men, just down from the woodlot, laughed mightily, straddling their chairs. Abe, though he's at least sixty and owns the highest hill in town, looked as if he'd worked hardest of all: his thick hands were creased with dirt and when he laughed sawdust shook out of his beard. Audie lives just in the valley, so she's always at Ma's. Her children were drawing backward alphabets over sheet after sheet of stationery on the floor. Ma had a roaring fire, for the first of September, though there was barely a chill. Everyone had a tumbler of scotch and a story, and the voices rose, overlapping, fragments flying from one conversation to the next, laughter careening. Stepping over the threshold, I nearly put my foot in a casserole.

"My strombolis!" Audie said. "Kate!"

I hadn't said I was coming. I wanted to slip in quietly.

"Kate? Oh, *Katie!*" Ma swooped across the room to embrace me as if her life depended on mine. She amplifies everything, to dazzle Abe, so I was welcomed now like a soldier home from the front. Everyone had to hug me, even Rolf, the new hired hand I'd never met before. Grace had been knitting in the firelight, and jumped up to clasp me so tight we bumped heads. Audie's children tumbled over themselves to reach me, each clinging to one leg.

I shrank away, afraid Ma would ask about Lawrence and I'd have to produce some stumbling explanation for the whole room, but of course she never thought of him. She doesn't care how I throw my life away as long as I'll spend some of it laughing with her.

"Well, Katie won't be so callous," she said to her audience. "After all, I was hanging by my thumbs." Retrieving Abe's eye, she returned to her story.

Audie read my pallor and moved over to give me the farthest

corner of the couch. "I'm sorry," she said. "It's been crazy the last few days." She always treats me with reverence and condescension mixed, as if I were at once too delicate and too exalted to be bothered with her mundane life. I left Brimfield, went to college, and lived by accidents of love, while she got married and had Tim and Lizzie right away. They bent luminous heads over their drawings at our feet.

"Lizzie," Audie said. "Go get your Aunt Kate a glass of scotch. You don't mind it straight, do you?" she asked me. "She can't do ice yet."

"I can so," Lizzie said, rolling her eyes in mock exasperation, stamping toward the kitchen, her fine blond hair swinging.

Ma's voice rose again. "Well, it seemed like I was hanging by my thumbs."

Audie shook her head, smiling; she thrives in a maelstrom. Besides the children and the housepet menagerie, and her regular and extra jobs, she's always peddling lobsters for the library fund or baking for the bereaved. She's a little spark plug, all duty and indignation, happiest when she's on her way down to give the PTA or the Zoning Board a piece of her mind. In a calm moment she'll get nervous, as if something must be secretly wrong.

"It's been crazy all week," she said. "You know about Grandma's flu?"

She knew I didn't; she was waiting to tell all. Though Ma and Grandma, as usual, weren't speaking, Ma had felt bound to nurse her and had taken Audie to mediate.

"God, she was sick," Audie said. "And of course she said if Ma called the doctor, she'd call the police."

"Is she better?" I asked. I didn't want to take a turn spending a night in that house, with its years of accumulated cooking odor and Grandma's little dried bouquets disintegrating everywhere.

Audie mistook my concern and rushed to reassure me. "She had hot peppers for breakfast, I think she's fine. But it was crazy! When I got home, the rabbits were loose . . ."

"They were in Daddy's boots!" Lizzie was back with my drink, which did have an ice cube, though in her race to join the story she'd sloshed most of the scotch away. "And, and . . ." She was almost too excited to speak, but in fear of being interrupted she took a breath and let her story spill. Toasters exploded, pressure cookers rocketed overhead while Lizzie, enthroned on her mother's lap, threw her quick hands up, gasping to show how she had gasped before, telling us all about it, as if the surging river of calamity would carry her through life on its crest.

". . . and Mommy couldn't go to her meeting, because the Town Hall burned down!"

This was the first thing I'd seen as I drove into town, and it gave me a cold thrill, like a nightmare. The Town Hall was built in 1751, and the sober ideals of that time had seemed to watch from its high windows over the length of Main Street. Now the great stone steps led to a roped-off pit, with an ancient, mossy graveyard beyond. The grocery, the pharmacy, and the church, abandoned, seemed scattered and small.

"Arson," said Audie matter-of-fact. She expects buildings to go off like Roman candles every now and again. "The third this summer."

"The fourth!" cried Ma. "Don't forget the Plaistow house."

"Now, we don't know that was arson," Abe said, but he hardly hoped to restrain her. Abe himself is so subdued that his every blink is subject to interpretation. Ma looked delighted to hear him speak.

"Please," she said, giddy on his attention. "There's a clear pattern. But they're hitting the wrong places. I've got some suggestions that would singe your eyebrows." She was speaking, as we all guessed, of the bank where she works as a part-time teller—though she's fit to be Loan Officer at least—and of my father's new house on the lake.

Grace knitted ominously. She's the youngest, and she had divided that summer, her last in college, evenly between my parents as always, working in the bookstore and walking home up the hill or down the lake road, according to the week. Justice herself doesn't clutch the scales tighter than Grace.

"It's not really funny," she said, sounding surprised to hear her own voice, shocked to hear it criticizing Ma. The fires were filling the town with fear. The arsonist seemed to crave a spectacle and was burning the largest buildings in town. After the Plaistows', Abe's is the biggest house.

"The caretaker died, you know," Grace said.

"You're right. I'm sorry, honey," Ma said, and sincerely, but under Abe's eye she can leave nothing plain. "I'm being silly. It's not only arson, it's murder, and it's horrible. The bastards should be torn limb from limb."

Why had I come here? At my house the worst noise is Lawrence turning another page. Yesterday I'd called him a pedant, clinging to his theories, afraid to put his feet down in the thick stream of life. I'd accused him of killing my youth with neglect. Now I remembered how spare and pure was the life in our clean-swept apartment, how free of false hopes, embarrassing ideas.

". . . drawn and quartered! Ripped on the rack!" cried my mother, pausing to take a sip.

"That's not what I meant," said Grace miserably. She glanced up for my support but, finding it, judged me as she judged herself: disloyal. She looked away. "Never mind," she said, pulling out a long row of stitches and starting again.

"I'm sorry, Sweetheart," Ma said. "I never mean to upset you, really I don't." She seemed to be pleading, and everyone was quiet, waiting for Grace to absolve her.

"I know," Grace said finally, wanting everything smooth. She strained for a true smile.

"I'm still a child, really, at heart," said Ma, relieved and airy, watching Abe. "That's why I annoy you all so. I'd be different if I could, really."

Abe drew heavily on his pipe, fighting his smile. He's not an immoderate man, but he's guilty of enjoying Ma far too much. Here this pleasure threatened its boundaries—we'd just seen his wife drive in. He put a hand to the small of his back and rose with a valedictory "Well . . ."

"Well . . ." echoed my mother, meaning that if Abe was leaving, the others ought to go home too. In a minute the room would be quiet. I'd have a bath. I'd tell my story.

But the party was not to be snuffed.

"Kate! I haven't talked to Katie!" protested Vinnie Duff, Abe's gardener, so that Rolf turned to eye me and repeated my name in a heavy, suggestive voice, as if in this roomful of delights I were a morsel he had yet to taste. Timmy climbed the bench to bang the piano until Abe's big black dog came out from beneath and stretched himself, baying along. Then the phone rang, from pure exuberance.

"Yes, Grandma," Audie shouted, answering with a finger in one ear. "Now you have to call a doctor. Yes, now! All right." She hung up and turned to us. "Pay attention, this is serious. Grandma has to go to the hospital." She was flushed with purpose, in command, and everyone sprang to her will as if we were firemen just waiting for a call.

I refused to worry: my family loves a crisis, a chance to drop all the tedious ordinary chores and surrender ourselves to emotion. Ma will manufacture an emergency whenever she's feeling dull.

Abe and Vinnie got clear of us, but Rolf was new on the hill. Everyone in Brimfield Valley can look up to see the neat fields at the Withans', the big white house, the apple trees. Rolf had expected to find Abe in a smoking jacket, and, in the chauffeur's quarters, a chauffeur. All evening he'd laughed in the wrong places, never sure how to take us. Carried away by Ma's attention, he'd tried to goose Grace, urging her to "loosen up." Now he threw back his shoulders and told us, from a pontifical height, that we had no need of doctors if Jesus was on our side.

Ma gave him a moment's polite smile, but he was off the subject.

"What about me?" she asked, still vamping, looking for our sympathy, our interest, or at least a laugh. "What about when I was sick? Did you find Grandma at my bedside? But now of course she expects . . ." Recalling what was expected, she gave a daughterly sigh. "I'll come with you, Audie," she said. "Kate, you and Grace meet us at the hospital."

"I'm sorry," Audie said to me over her shoulder. "It's been crazy all summer."

I felt a firm hand on my arm, so familiar I half expected to find Lawrence behind me, but when I turned, there was Rolf.

"Don't forget," he said, more threatening than kind. "You're in the palm of His hand."

"No, Mother. You may not 'die in peace,' " Ma said witheringly. She'd had to call the ambulance when Grandma refused to leave the house. Now Grandma lay before us on a gurney, in the corridor of the emergency room. They were pumping blood out of her stomach, dripping blood into her arm. Her face was thick and gray, her white hair stood on end, and all her softness, her sweet vagueness, was gone. Whether in peace or not, she was clearly dying. I told myself to look closely, to see what I could learn.

She tried to lift herself on an elbow, but failed, and gave me a rueful, cracking smile.

"Not a very good day for me," she said. She was neither frightened nor serene. This might have been another household predicament, a flooded washing machine or blown fuse. "But,

Katie," she said, and her voice filled with grandmotherly fondness, "your mother tells me you're going to have a baby."

Ma met my surprise with a whimsical shrug—no reason not to make promises now. I nodded to Grandma, smiling shyly, and reached for her hand, but there was a needle attached there.

"She'll name it for you," Ma said.

Grandma turned obstinately away from her.

"Even my last wish you disobey," she said, and the green masks came to wheel her away.

"It took three men to get her into the ambulance," Ma told the nurse, less vexed than proud.

"Was she unconscious?" The nurse was a preternaturally neat and smiling woman, and ready with compassion, but Ma gave a laughing shout.

"She was thrashing! She wants to 'die in peace'! Nothing less than death for her, no wretched little diseases."

Grandma has been suspicious of medicine since she was eight years old and the doctor was the only man in town with a car. He loomed up beside her in this gleaming contrivance as she walked home from school, helped her into the high seat like a lady, let her squeeze the horn and wave to her friends the whole length of Main Street to his office, where he chloroformed her and tried out another up-to-the-minute idea: a tonsillectomy.

"You're not to take any extraordinary measures to save her life," Audie said. "We promised."

The nurse smiled inscrutably.

" 'Extraordinary measures' indeed," said Ma. "She watches too much TV. Sit down, Audie, and stop worrying. I'll go hold her silly hand." She thrust Grandma's purse, a red straw clutch that must have had espadrilles to match, on me, sending me to fill out the forms.

Age? Seventy-nine. Address? Main Street. I fished for her driver's license and found the picture was a true one: it caught her smile that wishes to please and mocks the wish at once.

The others in my family, seeing the license, would have had to recount the time she got wedged in the drawbridge, or the time she sideswiped the mounted policeman's horse. I'm the only one of us who can fill out a simple form. Next of kin? My mad mother. My grandfather fell in love with a Parisian woman and never came home from the war. When we heard last year he was dead, Grandma said with a wistful laugh that she supposed she could stop waiting for a letter now. Religion? Irrelevant, I thought, but wrote *Catholic*, remembering Ma's tales of parochial school, though in fact there's no religion, no system for us at all. We're on the loosest of terms with God. We've been lucky all our lives, bobbed from mishap to mishap like a family of corks on a wild sea, so we trust of each accident the knowledge it will bring, the new vista it will spread before us. I looked up from the clipboard to see them consulting, comforting, tête-à-tête, relishing the adventure, but something of Lawrence's wintry spirit had settled into my bones, and I considered that our luck was only luck and would change.

"She's gonna be just fine!" Here was Ma's brother, Cap, in his big fur coat, just blown in with his equally fur-coated new wife, Rosetta. Cap believes in positive thinking, and it's his knack of making people think positively, about "no-risk bonds" and "guaranteed options," that obliged him to spend most of the last decade in Brazil. Still, he's Grandma's favorite, according to Ma. His rough, spreading face was radiant with corruption. His thunderous humor made the party.

"Wish we had olives," he said, unscrewing a small silver flask. "Doesn't seem like a real emergency, without an olive."

He bent a monstrous smile on Lizzie, who had been stroking the hem of his coat. She fell back, giggling, half in terror, but when her brother started laughing too, she drew herself up.

"We have to be quiet," she said, in a pious hush.

Yes, everything was to be savored: when the great automatic

doors puffed open to admit a priest whose robes billowed around him, Ma said, "Someone's dying," just as, when she closes the last window against a storm, she'll whistle softly and say, "Thar she blows."

We watched the priest make his way down the corridor, until he turned into Grandma's room.

"My God!" Ma was after him in an instant, the nurse behind her trying to tell her that last rites were a formality before any surgery at all.

"But she's an Episcopalian!" Ma wailed. The priest stood, hand raised, in the open door. Grandma lay in the center of the high, bright room, wrapped in a sheet. She opened her eyes. She sat straight up.

"Get out," she said. "Go." She pointed to the door with a hand that trailed a long tube.

The priest turned to us for an answer, but when he saw our faces, his fell.

"I'm sorry," Ma said, very kindly. "She's an Episcopalian."

"Katie, what did you tell them?" she asked me. "She only converted to please my father. She hasn't been Catholic for thirty years."

"She's so fickle!" I said. I apologized to the priest, but really I was pleased; I had added my voice to the family clamor. For a moment I had stepped inside their circle and felt its narcotic comfort—I was glad, suddenly, to be home, to be sharing the glory of disaster.

As the hours of the operation passed, I heard Ma tell the story of the priest again and again, to the nurse, to the other meek emergency patients, until I knew it would take its place with Grandma's drawbridge escapade and the time Ma got hung by her thumbs.

The hospital began to seem like Ma's living room. Grace spread cancer pamphlets facedown on the floor and knelt to draw scenes for the children: red barns and sheep fluffy as the clouds above, all pierced by the sun's yellow spines. Ma and Cap bickered over his flask: he accused her of swilling; she swore to everyone present that ever since childhood he'd been stingy and cruel. Audie got her casserole out of the car, and we picnicked under the "No Food or Drink" sign with our usual insouciance—who can deny us, all of us together?

Vulgar, I thought, and ostentatious, and typically self-absorbed. Are we so clever or lovely or even so kind that even our vices are charming? Surely, we would be struck dead any minute, for hubris. I feigned an interest in the bulletin board, though I hadn't eaten all day. When I turned around, the nurse was handing out plastic spoons. Everyone wanted a bite. Audie wrote out the recipe for the woman with the lacerated hand and took calls on the desk phone, which rang constantly, always for us. All the relatives were calling from pay phones: Aunt Georgie from her Clam Shack, my brother from his corner bar, Grandma's brother Arvid from a Labor Day flea market in Vermont. They'd get cut off, call back again, and again. "Yes," Ma kept saying, shouting to be heard over the surf, the ball game, the white-elephant hunting hordes. "Yes, a real priest!" A new batch of wounded—a whiplash and a broken toe—got to hear about the mounted police. By midnight everyone knew that Cap was Grandma's favorite, after Ma's father ran away.

" 'To lose one parent may be regarded as a misfortune. To lose both looks like carelessness.' " Ma spoke with an awful solemnity, as if she were quoting Thomas Jefferson and not Oscar Wilde. She wanted another laugh, but she had touched Audie's fears.

"If it's cancer, she'll never forgive me," Audie said. "I promised I wouldn't let them hurt her." She was rocking Timmy asleep, and she settled him again, squaring her shoulders to summon her ire. "I won't let them keep her here. They have no right . . ."

"Don't be silly," Ma said, still playing to the house. "Our family doesn't get cancer."

"Your father just died of it," I said.

"Well, you can hardly consider *him* one of the family."

Audie was crying. "We should never have made her come here," she sobbed. "All she wanted was to die in peace."

Lizzie, who had been coloring quietly, jumped up and flung herself into her mother's arms. Ma encircled them with one arm, Grace with the other. I watched from infinitely far away.

"Give me the flask, Cap," Ma said.

He held it away. "No, Lila Ann. It's my last sip."

"To think," Ma said. "She'll die loving you more than me."

Grace looked up from her knitting, which had grown spectacularly. "Is she going to die?" she asked.

"No," Cap said. "She's as tough as an old stewing chicken, and this is all the gin I have."

But when the nurse went to pick up a biopsy in the operating room, he said, "I knew it, it's cancer."

His new wife is Brazilian, wide and squat and generally eroded. She speaks very little English, so Cap feels free to call her "that toad I married," even when she's in the room. Now he hid his face against her shoulder and shook in the circle of her heavy arms as if he were sobbing too.

It was not cancer, however, but a mechanical disorder so common it had no name: her intestine had gotten a crimp in it and burst. The surgeon in his gown looked ten feet tall, but we hardly listened to his warnings. No complication, no trauma for us—we were beyond such things.

"I told you she'd be fine," Ma said.

"No, I told *you*," said Cap.

Behind him the nurse was taking another call, a man choking. The ambulance couldn't find the house.

"Turn right," the nurse repeated, but their radio wasn't working. Brimfield is all back roads winding up and down the hills. "Turn right, right!" she said, louder every time, but it seemed that only I could hear her.

By the exit, my family was at rest in the palm of His hand. Motley, disheveled, Audie and Grace each bearing a sleeping child, they willed the doors open and spilled out, all but singing, into the dark. I picked up the empty casserole and followed them. The summer air was back, soft and powerful.

"It'll be a tough recovery," Cap said, taking off his coat. "You'll have to stay with her, Lila Ann."

"You do it," Ma said. "You're the one she loves."

She was overcome with bitterness, now we were out of harm's way. "My little vacation with my daughters, completely spoiled," she said in the car, as if Grandma had nastily planned the whole thing.

I drowsed in the back seat, lulled by the old, familiar angers. We were safe at last, almost home. At the crest of Withans Hill three deer turned to watch us; Ma stopped the car, and we watched them too, in thrall to their beauty and fear. The floodlit church spire shone in the valley, with all Connecticut unfurled beyond. The dark houses stood with their maples, the hedgerows continued their orderly advance over the hills. I was certain the choking man must have been saved. Surely, everyone in that quiet landscape was safely asleep, in the arms of his beloved and the sight of God.

A few hours later the church burned to the ground. I was sleeping in the living room, so I could have looked out to see the flames, but when I heard the sirens I turned over and pulled the sheet up over my head. I woke in the morning to the bump of Abe's wheelbarrow along the back drive, sat up to see him resting on his rake like a figure out of Breughel, dwarfed by the tasseling corn.

It was one of those late-summer days that seem to swell with abundance, so that all life promises to ripen as simply as the apples on the trees. It was luxurious to miss Lawrence with the sun streaming through the screen door and the hot smell of the fields rising. Damning him, I longed for him. I wanted to see him stand with his coffee at the window, looking into the tangle of brush behind our apartment like a sailor scanning the sea. He has a stern, pure gaze that seems to see beyond the ordinary turmoils and obligations into a world of light, and people sometimes take him for a minister, but he's a history professor, or was until he came into his inheritance and retired. He was forty-five and filed to his essence, a bare moral wire, when I seduced him. I wanted to lift my arms and be borne up out of the family morass, to marry above my station.

The gods must have sent me to him for a joke! He had lived so deep in the world of abstraction that he claimed never to have touched silk or tasted ginger. When I brought home a bunch of red tulips, he stepped back in awe; as they opened in their vase, he would approach them shyly, lifting his hand beside their loose heads like a conductor urging a crescendo. After his years of austerity I was a wild extravagance, and if at first I delighted him, I soon became an embarrassment. He returned to his contemplations, reading hour by hour in his favorite chair, looking up only to take a judicious note. Nothing came up to his standards, including his own works, which, beyond pronouncing them "mortal indeed," he refused to mention. He did once compliment a phrase of mine, but in general he kept his face in his book as if he hated to look up and find me deviling the room. I tried to be braver, wiser, more grave, but nothing impressed him. Under his gloomy authority I felt I would wither away.

When I remembered my parents, my grandparents, the way they gave up on each other, I knew I should seize myself and persevere. I began to lecture Lawrence, eloquent as a prisoner addressing his cell wall. Marriage, I said, was a vocation; we must strive to build a temple between us, of simple, soaring lines. He'd give an impatient nod. Finally, recognition, which had been gathering, crystalized, and I said I had to leave.

"All right," he said, with a deep, acquiescent sigh. "What is it you want?"

I wanted laughter over nothing; the midnight recounting of dreams. I couldn't believe my life had ebbed so—that I had to ask for such things. "It's so simple," I said. "Plain dumb love."

A condescending smile flickered over his face. He'd taken a note or two on love. I waited for him to bring the whole of history down against me, to tell me again that no minor alliance counts for anything in this world of Declines and Falls. But something—my pure youth, I suppose—touched him.

"It's my fault," he said. His voice was dry and tender—he pitied me. "You got in with the wrong man, that's all, and you were too young to know."

His face, all pain, rebuked me. I'd crashed into his cloister— I'd been too young to care.

Now I felt plenty old, inoculated with his doubts—I would never belong among my own blithe people again. My anger was hardening to a cold, immovable weight, but even this seemed to unite us. Leaning back among the bedclothes, I considered that, like my mother and grandmother, I was lost to my marriage and that without Lawrence I would have to begin a long life alone.

"Coffee?" Vinnie Duff stood at the screen door. With his overalls, and the sun angling through his straw hat and curls, he looked like a scarecrow cut down from its stick. The first time I saw Vinnie, he was sailing backward past our window, riding the top rung of his ladder into the rhododendrons. He'd been painting the soffits at the wrong angle. When I ran out to help him, he propped himself on an elbow and said, "Now, when you're falling, the first thing to remember is save yourself, don't worry about the bucket."

Vinnie knows a lot about falling, but he's a terrible gardener.

Though he gave up law school for the simple life back in 1969, he still prizes reason over insight: he can't keep the roses from smelling of garlic, or save the scrofulous sunflowers, but he can always explain what went wrong.

"I'm in bed, Vinnie," I observed, but the shortest route to the garden is through Ma's living room, and they're all used to traipsing through as they please. Vinnie clomped into the bathroom to bring me a robe, turned his face resolutely to the wall as I put it on. Then he sat me down and told me, very gingerly, as if afraid I'd develop a crack, that Ma was back at the hospital where Grandma was dying again.

My hair was dirty and tangled, and I pulled it back with a piece of string while he made coffee. Without the camaraderie of crisis, death was its old black self again. I saw my grandmother's life shrunken—ruled, like all lives, by small hopes and fears, ended here arbitrarily after the years of schoolteaching, the years of duplicate bridge . . .

As I explained this to Vinnie, it devolved somehow into the story of Lawrence and me. Vinnie and I had never gotten far beyond the weather before, but I couldn't stop talking. He closed one eye to consider me as if I were a blighted rose.

"Well," he said finally, "doesn't death just show how small these little love worries are?" He looked extremely pleased with himself; he'd proved I ought to cheer up.

"No, Vinnie," I said. He gets everything backward. But I was not feeling discursive—my voice quavered.

"Wait, wait, Katie!" He jumped up in a panic, hoping to avert tears. "How about a tour of the garden?"

I followed him, repeating the flower names as he spoke them: cleome, portulaca, cosmos. I didn't want to make him uncomfortable, so I tried to be calm, but when we came to the astilbe, the word was so lush and strange—more lovely than the flower— I spoke it in a sob. He patted my back as if I were choking.

"I'm sorry," I said, to gain license to continue.

"Nothing to be sorry for," he said awkwardly, touching my shoulder.

"For heaven's sake, Vinnie," I said. "Put your arms around me."

He obeyed. His smell, of sweat and fresh earth, penetrated grief. Looking up, I caught his eye by accident. What you can learn in a half-second! Vinnie and I have known each other for years, and thoughts of him might have crossed my idle mind before, but in that instant we were suddenly a weedy Tristan and his sleep-sodden, tear-blotched Iseult. Flustered, I let go of him. Flummoxed absolutely, he loped off toward the woodshed, calling over his shoulder that he was sorry, he'd forgotten he had to meet Abe.

Grace cried in hiccups, in a corner of the windowless "quiet room," where the hospital, to spare us the indignity of public grief, had shut us up alone. The walls were blank green, the seats alternated orange and mauve. For solace there was a Bible; for nourishment, a jar of mints.

"What is it, honey?" I asked. Cap was with Grandma, Audie had taken the children to the lobby shop, and Ma was asleep across a row of seats, so the task of comfort fell to me.

"Nothing," Grace said, from the depths of a sob. "It's just, I don't know . . ."

She's always anxious, uncertain, as if she were on the brink of disaster somehow and the next flower she picked might rip the ground from beneath her. I get impatient—I tell her this world is all we have and we ought to take our chances here, rejoicing, but I can't persuade her to take heart.

"I never know what's wrong, Kate," she said. "That's what's wrong." I patted her shoulder but without much hope.

Ma woke by maternal instinct and felt blindly for her glasses.

"Who's crying?" she asked, thickly, pulling herself up and stumbling across the room to take Grace's other side.

"Now, Grandma's had a long, happy life," she began. I shook my head, knowing Grace mourned something far beyond this, but the old commonplaces, the old cadences, worked their old effect. Grace nodded acquiescence, wiping her eyes. Her knitting, a mass of rough, greenish stuff, spilled over her knees like a fisherman's mossy net.

"It's lovely," Ma said dryly. "What is it?" Over Grace's head she made a face: we all wonder why Grace can't, just one time, wear red.

"It doesn't matter," Grace said. "It's all screwed up."

"Honey, you do everything perfectly," Ma said, but this just prompted a new sob. Our little griefs, which will do circus tricks for the right audience, loomed up against us now we were all alone. Grace refused consolation, and Ma, having failed, started to cry too.

"I can't even help my own children," she said. Still weeping, Grace swore this wasn't true. Convinced mine was the purest sorrow, I opened the Bible, thinking to escape them, but Cap burst through the door.

"Nice, regular breathing!" he said.

"She's on a respirator, Cap," Ma told him.

"She's gonna be a brand-new old lady in no time flat," he said, with a broad wink at the wary Grace.

Ma blew her nose. "She's not a used car, Cap," she said.

Never mind, he told her. Even the economics would work out. We'd save hundreds a day if Grandma was released early. Uncle Arvid could take care of her—he'd been a medic in the Second World War.

"Is that what you told the doctors?" Ma said. Arvid saw too much in Europe, and he's been on lithium since V-E Day. He's an antique dealer now.

"Don't be silly, Lila Ann," said Cap with deafening assurance. "He can nurse her. You know he passed the postal exam."

"He quit the second day!" Ma said, but she caught herself.

146

"We don't need to get into this. Her blood pressure's almost nil now."

"Don't say that, Lila Ann," Cap said between his teeth. His first wife was killed in a car wreck, while he was in Brazil. We didn't know what name he was using, couldn't find him, so Grandma arranged the funeral. After he came home, he stuck close to her, and he wasn't going to let her go too.

Audie appeared in the doorway with the children, who carried new silver pinwheels like wands.

"We should have let her stay at home," she said. "Now she'll go to her grave hating me."

"Well, she never loved me at all," said Ma.

"She's not going to her grave," Cap said. "They promised they'd keep her alive."

"I'll pull the tubes myself," Audie wept.

Grace had dried her tears while the others squabbled, and I saw her summon courage again.

"We ought to call Daddy," she said. "We ought to let him know."

I laughed, God forgive me.

"Katie," Grace said. "He's one of the family."

Yes, but the last time Ma saw him, in the courthouse parking lot, she tried to run him over. After a decade of divorce she's still in a rage.

Lizzie blew a wicked gust into her pinwheel. "Grandma hates Grandpa, doesn't she?" she said.

"They have a difference of opinion," Audie began, but Ma laughed and swept the child up in her arms.

"You are such a vicious child!" she said, rocking her proudly, kissing her, while Lizzie beamed.

Grace and Audie and I look nothing alike—Grace is all angles, Audie's taut, and I tend toward the blowzy—but our eyebrows confirmed us as sisters now: all were raised. Lizzie leaned back in Ma's arms, pinwheel blazing, and everything came right side up again. By the time the nurse knocked to say Grandma was conscious, we felt her recovery was only our due.

Cap took it as proof he could sell anything.

"I told them!" he crowed at her bedside. "They didn't believe me, Ma."

Amid the thump and flutter of the machines Grandma opened a weary eye. Though her face showed mostly pain, she seemed to be asking a question, and after a few tries we guessed it.

"No," Ma said. "It wasn't cancer. You're fine." Grandma's face went calm.

"*Now* will you say I was right?" Ma asked. "*Now* are you glad we brought you?"

Grandma set her mouth in a stubborn line.

"I know how you'll remember this," Ma said. "This will be the time Cap saved your life."

"*Ma*," I said.

"Don't be ridiculous," Ma said. "I told her. She's fine."

And we tumbled, jubilant, into the big waiting room, like actors out from the curtain, almost expecting applause. Abe was there, as if Ma had conjured him, twisting his canvas fishing hat in his hand, chewing a dead pipe. He twinkled all over to see us, tamped his pipe as if to light it, but remembered the no-smoking sign. On the seat beside him was a silver ice bucket with his wife's monogram.

"Champagne!" Ma cried.

Alas, no. Rolf had cut off his hand with the chain saw, and Abe knew it would keep best on ice.

Thanks to this, the hand could be promptly reattached, once the microsurgeon flew in from New York. In forty-eight hours Rolf's fingertips were glowing a healthy pink, and they said he'd move his thumb by Halloween.

Now, Ma, said, we had to have champagne. There was everything to celebrate: Grandma was about to be released, and

Great-uncle Arvid was leaving the flea market early to come down and nurse her. Lizzie had gone forth to kindergarten, leaving Audie in tears at the bus. Grace shook out her knitting to reveal a sheath that fell straight from shoulder to hip to knee. She tugged at the hem in bitter frustration, pronouncing it uneven, wracked with flaws, but it became her absolutely. Regal and diffident, she boarded the bus to Boston with her many satchels and her bouquet of wild asters, bravely offering her ticket to be punched, turning in the door to smile goodbye, an angel of uncertainty.

Best of all, Abe's wife was marching on Washington, against nuclear arms. She would be spending the whole night away. Ma decided to give a party, just the two of us and Vinnie and Abe. All week she'd been lost in her sorrows, so I had yet to tell her about Lawrence, but as we rifled her closet for silk and satin, with the evening like a great city on the horizon, my marriage began to seem just another run-of-the-mill disaster, and I considered how I might fashion it into a tale.

"I've left Lawrence," I began, meaning to make it funny, but I felt dizzy suddenly, as if I were looking over a high cliff.

"Oh, Kate," Ma said. "Oh, honey, I'm so sorry." She had been holding up a blouse in the mirror, and she set it down for a minute, but it was the same blue as her eyes and she couldn't quite let it go.

"Well," she said to my reflection, "at least you only wasted three years. With me, it was twenty."

"I had to leave, Ma," I said, afraid I might start crying. "I couldn't stand it anymore, I . . ."

"I told all of you not to get married," she said. "Now, I wash my hands." She held up two necklaces: "Gold or pearls?"

"Gold," I said. I felt yanked back from the precipice, saved. "Flash before luster."

"That's my Katie," she said, looping them together over her head.

When Abe saw us in our finery, he went back across the driveway and returned with his wife's satin kimono over his jeans and a pointy Chinese hat. Vinnie had been haunting the second-hand stores and wore all his favorites: emerald jacket, orange tie, pants of emerald-and-orange plaid.

"Why no imagination?" he asked. "Why the same tired colors over and over again?" Vinnie and I had been awkward since our embrace in the garden, stranger to each other than if we'd never met. We'd gotten into each other's imagination. He kept arriving at the screen door, endlessly smiling, talking just to keep my attention. He brought me new facts shyly as if they were jewels: from the juice of the privet berry, I learned, the first mapmakers distilled their ink. Tropical earwigs come in violent colors and eat meat. That afternoon, impatient with entomology, I'd asked him what he wanted of love. "Comfort," he said, very uncomfortably. "Buy an armchair!" I told him. I preached transports of devotion, jabbing my finger into the air. "Love is the last frontier!" I said. Wanting to drink from his teacup, and deeply, I seized it so mightily I drenched us both. I tried to blot his shirt with a dish towel, but he kept backing away. Now, when he sat down at the picnic table beside me, he kept a little distance, afraid of what I might do.

The champagne cork shot off into a night of high, luminous clouds. We had damask on the table, Verdicchio in the ice bucket, Abe's crystal, and Vinnie's sweetest rose.

"I don't know," Ma said. "Why should it have been such a hard life?"

She seemed to ask in the name of science, but not even Vinnie could answer.

"They never loved me," she said. Grandma's resurrection had thrown things into sorry focus for her; she'd begun tabulating her troubles as if about to present a bill.

"They loved Cap," she said. "He was the son. I was the slave."

She deserved sympathy—her sorrows threatened at any moment to swallow her—but it was hard to weep for one who could call herself a slave in such round and ringing tones. We had finished the Verdicchio and opened a Côtes du Rhône; when no one answered her, Ma yanked the bottle from the bucket to pour another round. I winced as she plunged it back into the ice, remembering Rolf's hand.

"I thought my father loved me, but clearly I was wrong," Ma said. "I thought if I was patient, my husband . . . I thought if I gave him time . . ." She stopped. She had opened too deep a wound.

Vinnie commenced disputation: "But I'm sure your mother loves you."

"Unwittingly," Ma said. "Only because she's my mother. Not in any real way."

"You must feel loved here?" Vinnie tried again.

She looked straight into Abe's eyes. "Must I?" she asked, from a bibulous mist. "Must I really?" He said nothing, holding her gaze.

"Forgive her," I said to Vinnie. I was mortified.

"Nothing to forgive," he said stoutly.

Abe continued intent on Ma, like a man staring into a flame. Drink made him stiffer and more formal as it unloosed the last of her stays. Meditatively, never taking his eyes from Ma, he held a cork in the candle flame and began, with slow, meticulous strokes, to black her face.

She kept perfectly still, lifting her chin, watching his eyes.

"Now I'll be beautiful," she said. "I've always wanted to be beautiful. Don't I look beautiful, Katie?"

She looked like a panther in the woods, her eyes burning.

"Fit to kill," I said.

"Go to hell." She tipped backward over the bench so that the soles of her feet showed where her face had been. Abe put the cork to the candle again and started to black them, toe by toe. Suppose his wife got home early? She might decide they needed a chauffeur after all. Ma couldn't afford to pay rent— where would she go?

"So," I said, hoping to rescue her, "who's the arsonist?"

They would know, even if the police didn't—the town was too small for a mystery. Already I'd heard how he did it: he opened electric meters and crossed wires, or yanked the propane lines, freeing the captive forces to wreak their natural havoc. Vinnie named as the culprit a big kid from the valley who'd been at school with me. It was rumored he'd singed his hair in the Town Hall fire. His girlfriend had trimmed it but then discovered he was unfaithful, and was showing the clippings around.

"Unfaithful," came Ma's wondering voice from below. "Maybe he loved them both. Maybe his heart is broken."

"Ma," I said, but Abe only smiled. Finishing her feet, he joined her upside down.

"I've blackened your soles," he said.

"Forgive them," I said to Vinnie, but he was paying them no attention. He'd been watching the gold beads flash at my throat, and when I spoke he looked guiltily away. We'd discussed celestial navigation, and I asked if he wanted to go look at the stars. No, he said, scandalized—it was getting late. Abe stood up at this and dusted himself, saying he couldn't think where the time had gone.

Ma spent the night passed out on the bathroom floor. She was against the door, so I went around to the window to check on her. She mastered a giggle and, with the most solemn sincerity, apologized.

"Don't be silly," I said. "You didn't seem foolish at all. Good night, I love you."

"No," she said, with deep satisfaction. "Nobody loves me." Then, all sleepy sweetness, by motherly rote: "I love you, sweetheart. Sleep tight."

I squatted in back of the arbor to pee. The night was awash

with stars. I fell asleep inventing harangues for Lawrence, lectures on the small acts of courage and generosity, the everyday absolution of love. I dreamed of Vinnie Duff, with his plain surprised face, his straw curls crazily bobbing. When he moved to kiss me, I fell back into space, but fear flashed to awe and as I woke with the dreamer's start I knew it was glory, to be falling.

In the morning I brought Ma her breakfast in bed: two aspirins and a cup of tea. She lifted her head just enough to swallow and sank back against the pillow with a weak moan. We heard the front door open, then the back. Abe had gone through to the garden with a bucket of mulch. In the center of the living room table he'd left a tiny vase of love-in-a-mist.

"No," Ma said, when I said I'd bring it into her. "Leave it where he put it. I can get up."

One hand to her forehead, the other at the neck of her dressing gown, she leaned in the doorway and smiled until I thought she'd cry.

"Don't you see?" she said. "It's his way of saying he loves me."

"Why doesn't he just tell you?" I asked.

"He doesn't have to," she said, as if I were terribly obtuse. "Let's boil some eggs. I'm starving."

While the eggs bumped and knocked in a pot on the stove, she traced a looping "I Love You" in the film of grease on the cabinet door. She washed it with ammonia and scrubbed it with bleach, trying to erase it, but the words kept shining.

"Katie," she said. "He'll see it. He'll *know*."

"Believe me," I said, "no one ever knows what anyone else means by that."

She wasn't attending. "I suppose it's a sign," she said, sighing prettily. "You can't undo love."

Her hangover cured, she strode up Grandma's walk that

afternoon like a banker, still in her black silk suit from work, her jug of scotch like a briefcase at her side.

Grandma wore an electric-blue silk suit with gold scarf.

"Saks Fifth Avenue," she said with a coy blink. "Two-fifty at The Bargain Box." She was triumphant now, gazing beatifically over her family, immortal at seventy-nine. She sighed over the handsome surgeon, contriving ways to see him again, but when Audie, who was still suffering, asked if she'd forgiven them for taking her to the hospital, she returned a final and capricious "No."

"In retrospect we just should have strangled you," Ma said.

We were all in the grandest high spirits. We had faced death; death couldn't face us. Lizzie, still in her tutu from ballet, circled the room in lopsided pirouettes, nearly toppling Uncle Arvid, who tapped his hearing aid and steadied himself on his cane. Driving down the night before, he had turned off the road into the woods and broken an axle on a stone wall.

"There used to be a road there," he kept explaining.

"You're getting senile, Arvid," Ma said sadly.

"What, Lila Ann?" He had picked up a silver-framed photograph of her as a child, alone in a rowboat like a tiny refugee.

"Nice," he said. "Sterling."

"The picture of a little girl who wasn't loved," said Ma. Her voice had a reckless edge, suddenly, and I braced myself. Seeing Grandma about to slip away, she had wanted to yank her back, to demand an apology. Now she had her wish, and I wasn't sure what she would say. Arvid looked up at her in surprise.

"We all loved you, Lila Ann," he said.

"You're getting senile," Ma snapped. "It was Cap you all loved. The son." Arvid was six inches shorter than she, a poor adversary. She leaned down and shouted into his ear. "Remember?"

He reeled backward.

"And don't fall," she said, as if he had stumbled to provoke her. She seized his elbow.

154

"Now, Lila," Grandma said, but she was too pleased with life to be truly grieved. "Don't be silly. I loved you both. And where *is* Cap? He was so good to me when I was in the hospital."

Her voice was foolish with fondness. Cap, we told her, was at an IRS hearing. Ma drew herself up with a delicate harumph, and when Audie and I returned little harumphing smiles, she was content.

"Katie," Ma said, "will you promise to shoot me if I start to act like her?"

I promised, and with a glance Audie promised me that she'd shoot me if I ever got like Ma, who, mollified, was pouring juice for the children, scotch for us.

"Just a thimbleful," said Grandma.

"You don't get any!" Ma said. "A gallon of blood they took out of you, Mother, a gallon."

But weights and measures had no place here. It was becoming a story. Even Lizzie, who sat in Audie's lap straight as a music box figurine, had been hoarding details.

"A whole gallon!" she said, her eyes alight. "And we ate supper in the emergency room. And Aunt Katie called the priest."

"I blame you, Kate, for saving her," Ma said. "You got her pulse going."

I was becoming a heroine. How large our lives looked, with the ambulance screaming, the priest's flying robes!

"Kate, I suppose you know I'm president of the Episcopal Churchwomen," Grandma said, rearranging her skirt.

"That election was rigged," said Ma. "And we have to go."

"No, Lila, when your poor mother just got out of the hospital?" Grandma said. "I need you to stay, at least until Cap comes."

"Why should I?" Ma said. "Would you have stayed for me?"

The truth was, we had to get home before Abe's stopping-by time, and I wanted to see Vinnie too. Ma drove like mad, and we sprang out of the car to range ourselves nonchalantly in the yard, Audie hiking her skirt to take the last sun while the children played a game of feints and whispers in the long grass. Who could resist having a drink with us? But Abe only passed through, on his way to the garden. His wife was bringing some of the nuclear ladies to tea. He cut a sheaf of zinnias and cosmos, limping more heavily than usual, looking sheepish, as if he ought to give the flowers to Ma.

"That was a lovely dinner," he said, with a slight bow.

"Come back tonight," said my wicked mother. Shrewd and wistful, mostly amused, he declined.

Ma watched his back in fond disappointment as he headed under the arbor, back to his wife.

"No love-in-a-mist for the nuclear ladies," she said, gloating, turning her glass as if she might read her fortune in the scotch.

And, as if she had seen a happy fate there, she looked up smiling.

"Life is so wonderful," she said. All the world's insults were forgotten at the sight of Abe's crooked gait, even if he was walking away.

"Imagine Grandma asking for a thimbleful of scotch," Ma said. "When last week all she wanted was to die in peace. You were right, Kate, I would have been sad if she'd died. I suppose it's always sad."

Even this comforted her. "We lead a charmed life!" she went on. "Look at this . . ." She spread an arm across the sweep of our borrowed abundance: a golden twilit haze hung over the orchard, which seemed to be our own orchard, we loved it so. Vinnie came whistling up the path, arms full of gigantic zucchini.

"You don't want to overfertilize," he instructed. I smiled up into his eyes, holding out my arms as if these were holy vegetables, but the phone started ringing and I had to run inside.

"Kate?" Lawrence's voice cracked. It might not have been used for days.

"How are you?" I spoke carefully, afraid my heart would fly out of my mouth. "What's happening there?" Vinnie had followed me in with the zucchini but, hearing my tone, went back outside.

"Nothing." There was a long pause while Lawrence tried to think of some news. "*The Ottoman Centuries* came in," he said. He'd been waiting for this, on interlibrary loan. Then, as if he hoped I wouldn't hear him: "I miss you."

"I miss you too." This was the incorrect answer, but his voice sounded like home to me. I'd have held the phone in silence all day if he was on the other end.

"How's the weather?" I asked.

"Hot. When you come home, we'll go for a swim, eh?"

"We will?" He knew I wasn't coming home.

"If you like," he said. I heard volumes of tender apology. Imagine Lawrence swimming! Tears pricked at my throat, my eyes. He was all talk now, bubbling over with relief, since I hadn't said I wasn't coming home. He told me how Byzantium crumbled, how the sultans charged the gates of Vienna . . .

"If they'd won, you'd be wearing a chador!" he said.

He knows so many perils! And he's entrusted himself to me. I felt I had gifts to bring home to him, jewels of vanity and self-pity and overweening pride. I wanted to tell him how we had faced death with linked arms. On the cabinet, Ma's indelible valentine shone.

In the garden she was screaming. I ran out to find her sprawled among the eggplants, gasping with laughter. Everyone was bent around her, inspecting the three drops of blood welling from her evenly punctured foot. She had stepped on Abe's rake, and the handle had come up and broken her glasses in two.

"These things only happen to us!" she said, as if this were a blessing.

"I know," I said. If it pleases us to imagine ourselves remarkable, why should we not? Even I felt exemplary all of a sudden, just to be standing on top of that hill.

"We'd better get you to a doctor," Audie said, returned to herself and ready for a new saga. "A puncture wound's the worst kind." She turned to me with an enormous, apologetic sigh. "I'm sorry, Katie, it's been crazy all year."

"Did you say the doctor?" Lizzie stopped still, hands on tutu'd hips. "Is this an emergency?"

"No," began judicious Vinnie, for whom I felt a sweet nostalgia already, but Ma interrupted.

"Of course it's an emergency," she said. "Don't listen to him."

Then she said, tartly, "See?"—because the sirens in the valley had begun to howl. I tried to resist it, but they filled me with a wild fear and joy.

"Emergency!" Lizzie cried, and she leapt, en pointe, through the squash vines, alive in the world of dangers, singing, "Emergency, emergency!" with her whole red heart.